W0246629

PENGUIN BOOKS

WHEN DARKNESS FALLS AND OTHER STORIES

Ruskin Bond's first novel, *The Room on the Roof*, written when he was seventeen, received the John Llewellyn Rhys Memorial Prize in 1957. Since then he has written a number of novellas, essays, poems and children's books, many of which have been published by Penguin. He has also written over 500 short stories and articles that have appeared in magazines and anthologies. He received the Sahitya Akademi Award in 1992, the Padma Shri in 1999 and the Padma Bhushan in 2014.

Ruskin Bond was born in Kasauli, Himachal Pradesh, and grew up in Jamnagar, Dehradun, New Delhi and Shimla. As a young man, he spent four years in the Channel Islands and London. He returned to India in 1955. He now lives in Landour, Mussoorie, with his adopted family.

WHEN DARKNESS FALLS
AND OTHER STORIES

RUSKIN BOND

PENGUIN BOOKS

An imprint of Penguin Random House

PENGUIN BOOKS

USA | Canada | UK | Ireland | Australia
New Zealand | India | South Africa | China | Singapore

Penguin Books is part of the Penguin Random House group of companies
whose addresses can be found at global.penguinrandomhouse.com

Published by Penguin Random House India Pvt. Ltd
4th Floor, Capital Tower 1, MG Road,
Gurugram 122 002, Haryana, India

Penguin
Random House
India

First published by Penguin Books India 2001

ISBN 9780141006833

Printed at Manipal Technologies Limited, India

www.penguin.co.in

Contents

Introduction

Although most of the stories in this collection were written in recent months, several are set in the period of my boyhood and youth—the semi-autobiographical stories of life in my grandmother's home in Dehra Dun, and the later freelancing years of 'Living Without Money'.

We are creatures of circumstance. If our genes have shaped our biological make-up, our environment has shaped the development of our natures. Nostalgia is an attempt to preserve that which was good in the past. But my tales are not simply about nostalgia. They are about how the process of growing up has made us what we are today. Would I have been a different sort of person if I had grown up in Scotland or Zanzibar instead of Dehra Dun or the Simla hills? Perhaps not, but the people I'd have met along the way would have been very different, and it's other people who often influence our development and the directions our lives take.

'When Darkness Falls' is fiction, but as a boy I did know of a man who never left his room and whose meals were left outside his door. The reason was different. The man was a leper, and in those days lepers were outcasts of society, as they still are in parts of the country. Markham is a different sort of outcast, but he too is a creature of circumstance.

Would Susanna have set out to destroy her husbands if some childhood experience had not turned her against men in general? Or was it simply in her nature to want to dominate the opposite sex? Some people climb mountains for pleasure; others climb in order to conquer peaks. A friend of my youth, who was sexually impotent, went on to conquer peak after peak. Each one, he confided, was like conquering a woman.

A word about the genesis of 'When Darkness Falls'. It has echoes of the *Phantom of the Opera*, a film which I greatly enjoyed as a boy. Claude Rains as the crazed genius underplayed the role superbly, while Nelson Eddy's rich baritone lent authenticity to the operatic scenes. But Markham is not a crazed genius. He is normal as you or me, perhaps more so. His disfigurement is accidental. How would we have reacted in similar circumstances? Hidden from the world like Markham, or confronted it with half a face?

Not an easy choice, my friend.

*

Last week, a young lady who interviewed me for one of those ephemeral websites, asked me if I had any regrets in life.

I thought long and hard about it but couldn't really put my finger on any specific or major regret, except that I would have liked to have been kinder and more considerate to some people, and tougher and more unyielding to others. A regret that is common to most of us, I think. But that apart, and my failure to make it to Torquay United's football 'B' team, I don't think I have anything to complain about.

Would I have been more successful if I had stayed on in England as a young man? A question that's often put to me.

Honestly, I don't think so. My inspiration, or subject matter if you like, has always come from my Indian background and experience—my relationship to people, the landscape, the atmosphere. The West never affected me in the same way. I spent almost four years in the UK, but very little of that time or experience made any impression on me, either as a person or as a writer.

If I had stayed on in England, what would there have been to write about? I had gone there steeped in English literature, my mind full of Victorian and Georgian novelists and poets, but the reality of post-War London was very different from the world of Pickwick and the Drones Club. My reality was India, and I needed more of India and less of England for my literary aspirations to be satisfied. And so it was back to India, and a small flat with a balcony overlooking a busy road in a small town, and the stories and essays poured forth even if they weren't being paid for; but this was what I'd always wanted, it was freedom, and I wasn't going to give it up for a job in Australia or a career in advertising. There was no uprooting me from the soil in which I was so well rooted. And besides, my readers were *here*.

My interlocutor's next question came out of the blue. Did I ever regret not having married?

This was something I had never really given much thought, and now I was being forced to consider it and voice an opinion. And I had to admit that I had no regrets about staying single. Marriage is a fine institution, I'm sure, and most of my friends are married people, making a valuable contribution to the continuity of the human race; but I am basically a selfish character, and I would hate to give up the independence I have enjoyed for the greater part of my life. In this respect I am a bit like P.G. Wodehouse's Bertie Wooster, terrified of being mothered or fussed over by some large imposing female, such as the athletic Honoria Glossop. I find the world full of Honoria Glossops. I don't have a Jeeves to protect me, but I have Prem and *his* family, and they look after me like no one has ever been looked after before. I am all for the joint family, especially as I am the main beneficiary of this one.

And do I regret having given up the city for the hills?

An emphatic 'No'. For the choice was a deliberate one. I can write almost anywhere—even a railway compartment will do—and I chose the hills for the purpose of *living* rather than as a congenial place for writing. The mountains make a man realize just how insignificant he is. At the same time, they allow one to remain an individual instead of being swallowed up in the crowd. I enjoy visiting cities; I enjoy travelling over the plains of India; I am fascinated by the desert; but it is always good to come home to the hills.

'Who goes to the Hills, goes to his Mother,' wrote Kipling in one of his more sublime moments.

So no regrets at all? Wouldn't I have liked to make more money, been published more widely? Certainly, but not at the expense of the lifestyle that has brought me considerable contentment and, at times, happiness. To be lionized in literary circles here and abroad must be very satisfying for a certain kind of writer, but I have always worked in isolation, far removed from the literary crowd, and I am ill-at-ease at intellectual cocktail parties. The cocktails usually run away with the intellect.

And if I could live my life all over again, would I do things differently, try to be someone else?

I don't think so, because a writer has to live and write within his nature, and this is what I have done and this is what I would do again. I'd like to have spent more time, a few more years, with my father who was snatched away while I was still a boy; and I suppose that would have altered things, and the opportunities would have been different. But it was not to be. That was chance, not choice. Chance gives, and takes away, and gives again.

No, given the opportunity to lead my life all over again, I wouldn't change much. Not even my purple socks.

When Darkness Falls

Markham had for many years lived alone in a small room adjoining the disused cellars of the old Empire Hotel in one of our hill stations. His Army pension gave him enough money to pay for his room rent and his basic needs, but he shunned the outside world—by daylight, anyway—partly because of a natural reticence and partly because he wasn't very nice to look at.

While Markham was serving in Burma during the War, a shell had exploded near his dugout, tearing away most of his face. Plastic surgery was then in its infancy, and although the doctors had done their best, even going to the extent of giving Markham a false nose, his features were permanently ravaged. On the few occasions that he had walked abroad by day, he had been mistaken for someone in the final stages of leprosy and been given a wide berth.

He had been given the basement room by the hotel's elderly estate manager, Negi, who had known Markham in the years before the War, when Negi was just a room-boy.

Markham had himself been a youthful assistant manager at the time, and he had helped the eager young Negi advance from room-boy to bartender to office clerk. When Markham took up a wartime commission, Negi rose even further. Now Markham was well into his late sixties, with Negi not very far behind. After a post-War, post-Independence slump, the hill station was thriving again; but both Negi and Markham belonged to another era, another time and place. So did the old hotel, now going to seed, but clinging to its name and surviving on its reputation.

'We're dead, but we won't lie down,' joked Markham, but he didn't find it very funny.

Day after day, alone in the stark simplicity of his room, there was little he could do except read or listen to his short-wave transistor radio; but he would emerge at night to prowl about the vast hotel grounds and occasionally take a midnight stroll along the deserted Mall.

During these forays into the outer world, he wore an old felt hat, which hid part of his face. He had tried wearing a mask, but that had been even more frightening for those who saw it, especially under a street lamp. A couple of honeymooners, walking back to the hotel late at night, had come face to face with Markham and had fled the hill station the next day. Dogs did not like the mask, either. They set up a furious barking at Markham's approach, stopping only when he removed the mask; they did not seem to mind his face. A policeman returning home late had accosted Markham, suspecting him of being a burglar, and snatched off the mask. Markham, sans nose, jaw and one eye, had smiled a crooked smile, and the policeman had taken to his heels. Thieves and goondas he could handle; not ghostly apparitions straight out of hell.

Apart from Negi, only a few knew of Markham's existence. These were the lower-paid employees who had grown used to him over the years, as one gets used to a lame dog or a crippled cow. The gardener, the sweeper, the dhobi, the night chowkidar, all knew him as a sort of presence. They did not look at him. A man with one eye is said to have the evil eye, and one baleful glance from Markham's single eye was enough to upset anyone with a superstitious nature. He had no problems with the menial staff, and he wisely kept away from the hotel lobby, bar, dining room and corridors—he did not want to frighten the customers away; that would have spelt an end to his own liberty. The owner, who was away most of the time, did not know of his existence; nor did his wife, who lived in the east wing of the hotel, where Markham had never ventured.

The hotel covered a vast area, which included several unused buildings and decaying outhouses. There was a Beer Garden, no longer frequented, overgrown with weeds and untamed shrubbery. There were tennis courts, rarely used; a squash court, inhabited by a family of goats; a children's playground with a broken see-saw; a ballroom which hadn't seen a ball in fifty years; cellars which were never opened; and a billiard room, said to be haunted.

As his name implied, Markham's forebears were English, with a bit of Allahabad thrown in. It was said that he was related to Kipling on his mother's side; but he never made this claim himself. He had fair hair and one grey-blue eye. The other, of course, was missing.

His artificial nose could be removed whenever he wished, and as he found it a little uncomfortable he usually took it off when he was alone in his room. It rested on his bedside table, staring at the ceiling. Over the years it had acquired a character of its own and those (like Negi) who had seen it looked upon it with a certain amount of awe. Markham avoided looking at himself in the mirror, but sometimes he had to shave one side of his face, which included a few surviving teeth. There was a gaping hole in his left cheek. And after all these years, it still looked raw.

*

When it was past midnight, Markham emerged from his lair and prowled the grounds of the old hotel. They belonged to him, really, as no one else patrolled them at that hour—not even the night chowkidar, who was usually to be found asleep on a tattered sofa outside the lounge.

Wearing his old hat and cape, Markham did his rounds.

He was a ghostly figure, no doubt, and the few who had glimpsed him in those late hours had taken him for a supernatural visitor. In this way the hotel had acquired a reputation for being haunted. Some guests liked the idea of having a resident ghost; others stayed away.

On this particular night Markham was more restless than usual, more discontented with himself in particular and with the world in general; he wanted a little change—and who wouldn't in similar circumstances?

He had promised Negi that he would avoid the interior of the hotel as far as possible; but it was midsummer, the days were warm and languid, the nights cool and balmy, and he felt like being in the proximity of other humans even if he could not socialize with them.

And so, late at night, he slipped out of the passage to his cellar room and ascended the steps that led to the old banquet hall, now just a huge dining room. A single light was burning at the end of the hall. Beneath it stood an old piano.

Markham lifted the lid and ran his fingers over the keys. He could still pick out a tune, although it was many years since he had played for anyone or even for himself. Now at least he could indulge himself a little. An old song came back to him and he played it softly, hesitantly, recalling a few words:

> *But it's a long, long time, from May to December,*
> *And the days grow short when we reach September . . .*

He couldn't remember all the words, so he just hummed a little as he played. Suddenly, something came down with a crash at the other end of the room. Markham looked up, startled. The hotel cat had knocked over a soup tureen that had been left on one of the tables. Seeing Markham's tall, shifting shadow on the wall, its hair stood on end. And with a long, low wail it fled the banquet room.

Markham left too, and made his way up the carpeted staircase to the first floor corridor.

Not all the rooms were occupied. They seldom were, these days. He tried one or two doors, but they were locked. He walked to the end of the passage and tried the last door. It was open.

Assuming the room was unoccupied, he entered it quietly. The lights were off, but there was sufficient moonlight coming through the large bay window with its view of the mountains. Markham looked towards the large double bed and saw that it was occupied. A young couple lay there, fast asleep, wrapped in each other's arms. A touching sight! Markham smiled bitterly. It was over forty years since anyone had lain in his arms.

There were footsteps in the passage. Someone stood outside the closed door. Had Markham been seen prowling about the corridors? He moved swiftly to the window, unlatched it, and stepped quickly out on to the landing abutting the roof. Quietly he closed the window and moved away.

Outside, on the roof, he felt an overwhelming sense of freedom. No one would find him there. He wondered why he hadn't thought of the roof before. Being on it gave him a feeling of ownership. The hotel, and all who lived in it, belonged to him.

The lights from a few skylights, and the moon above, helped him to move unhindered over the sloping, corrugated old tin roof. He looked out at the mountains, striding away into the heavens. He felt at one with them.

The owner, Mr Khanna, was away on one of his extended trips abroad. Known to his friends as the Playboy of the Western World, he spent a great deal of his time and money in foreign capitals: London, Paris, New York, Amsterdam. Mr Khanna's wife had health problems (mostly in her mind) and seldom travelled, except to visit godmen and faith-healers. At this point in time she was suffering from insomnia, and was pacing about her room in her dressing-gown, a loose-fitting garment that did little to conceal her overblown figure; for inspite of her many ailments, her appetite for everything on the menu card was undiminished. Right now she was looking for her sleeping tablets. Where on earth had she put them? They were not on her bedside table; not on the dressing table; not on the bathroom shelf. Perhaps they were in her handbag. She rummaged in a drawer, found and opened the bag, and extracted a strip of Valium. Pouring herself a glass of water from the bedside carafe, she tossed her head back, revealing several layers of chin. Before she could swallow the tablet, she saw a face at the skylight. Not really a face. Not a human face, that is. An empty eye-socket, a wicked grin, and a nose that wasn't a nose, pressed flat against the glass.

Mrs Khanna sank to the floor and passed out. She had no need of the sleeping tablet that night.

*

For the next couple of days Mrs Khanna was quite hysterical and spoke wildly of a wolf-man or Rakshas who was pursuing her. But no one—not even Negi—attributed the apparition to Markham, who had always avoided the guests' rooms.

The daylight hours he passed in his cellar room, which received only a dapple of late afternoon sunlight through a narrow aperture that passed for a window. For about ten minutes the sun rested on a framed picture of Markham's mother, a severe-looking but handsome woman who must have been in her forties when the picture was taken. His

7

father, an Army captain, had been killed in the trenches at Mons during the first World War. His picture stood there, too; a dashing figure in uniform. Sometimes Markham wished that he, too, had died from his wounds; but he had been kept alive, and then he had stayed dead-alive all these years, a punishment maybe for sins and excesses committed in some former existence. Perhaps there was something in the theory or belief in Karma, although he wished that things could even out a little more in *this* life—why did we have to wait for the next time around? Markham had read Emerson's essay on the law of compensation, but that didn't seem to work either. He had often thought of suicide as a way of cheating the fates that had made him, the child of handsome parents, no better than a hideous gargoyle; but he had thrust the thought aside, hoping (as most of us do) that things would change for the better.

His room was tidy—it had the bare necessities—and those pictures were the only mementoes of a past he couldn't forget. He had his books, too, for he considered them necessities—the Greek philosophers, Epicurus, Epictetus, Marcus Aurelius, Seneca. When Seneca had nothing left to live for, he had cut his wrists in his bathtub and bled slowly to death. Not a bad way to go, thought Markham; except that he didn't have a bathtub, only a rusty iron bucket.

Food was left outside his door, as per instructions; sometimes fresh fruit and vegetables, sometimes a cooked meal. If there was a wedding banquet in the hotel, Negi would remember to send Markham some roast chicken or pillau. Markham looked forward to the marriage season with its lavish wedding parties. He was a permanent though unknown wedding guest.

After discovering the freedom of the Empire's roof, Markham's nocturnal excursions seldom went beyond the hotel's sprawling estate. As sure-footed as when he was a soldier, he had no difficulty in scrambling over the decaying rooftops, moving along narrow window ledges, and leaping from one landing or balcony to another. It was late summer, and guests often left their windows open to enjoy the pine-scented breeze that drifted over the hillside. Markham was no voyeur, he was really too insular and subjective a person for that form of indulgence; nevertheless, he found it fascinating to observe people in their unguarded moments: how they preened in front of mirrors, or talked to themselves, or attended to their little vanities, or sang or scratched or made love (or tried to), or drank themselves into a stupor. There were many men (and a few women) who preferred drinking in their rooms to drinking in the bar—it was cheaper, and they could get drunk and stupid without making fools of themselves in public.

One of those who enjoyed a quiet tipple in her room was Mrs Khanna. A vodka with tomato juice was her favourite drink. Markham was watching her soak up her third Bloody Mary when the room telephone rang and Mrs Khanna, receiving some urgent message, left her room and went swaying down the corridor like a battleship of yore.

On an impulse, Markham slipped in through the open window and crossed the room to the table where the bottles were arranged. He felt like having a Bloody Mary himself. It was years since he'd had one; not since that evening at New Delhi's Imperial, when he was on his first leave. Now a little rum during the winter months was his only indulgence.

Taking a clean glass, he poured himself three fingers of vodka and drank it neat. He was about to pour himself another drink when Mrs Khanna entered the room. She stood frozen in her tracks. For there stood the creature of her previous nightmare, the half-face wolf-demon, helping himself to her vodka!

Mrs Khanna screamed. And screamed again.

Markham made a quick exit through the window and vanished into the night. But Mrs Khanna would not stop screaming—not until Negi, half the staff, and several guests had entered the room to try and calm her down.

*

Commotion reigned for a couple of days. Doctors came and went. Policemen came and went. So did Mrs Khanna's palpitations. She insisted that the hotel be searched for the maniac who was in hiding somewhere, only emerging from his lair to single her out for attention. Negi kept the searchers away from the cellar, but he went down himself and confronted Markham.

'Mr Markham, sir, you must keep away from the rooms and the main hotel. Mrs Khanna is very upset. She's called in the police and she's having the hotel searched.'

'I'm sorry, Mr Negi. I did not mean to frighten anyone. It's just that I get restless down here.'

'If she finds out you're living here, you'll have to go. She gives the orders when Mr Khanna is away.'

'This is my only home. Where would I go?'

'I know, Mr Markham, I know. I understand. But do others? It unnerves them, coming upon you without any warning. Stories are going around . . . Business is bad enough without the hotel getting a reputation for strange goings-on. If you must go out at night, use the rear gate and stick to the forest path. Avoid the Mall road. Times have changed, Mr Markham. There are no private places any more. If you have to leave, you will be in the public eye—and I know you don't want that . . .'

'No, I can't leave this place. I'll stick to my room. You've been good to me, Mr Negi.'

'That's all right. I'll see that you get what you need. Just keep out of sight.'

So Markham confined himself to his room for a week, two weeks, three, while the monsoon rains swept across the hills, and a clinging mist gave everything a musty, rotting smell. By mid-August, life in a hill station can become quite depressing for its residents. The absence of sunshine has something to do with it. Even strolling along the Mall is not much fun when a thin, cloying drizzle is drifting into your face. No wonder some take to drink. The hotel bar had a few more customers than usual, although the carpet stank of mildew and rats' urine.

Markham made friends with a shrew that used to visit his room. Shrews have poor eyesight and are easily caught and killed. But as they are supposed to bring good fortune, they were left alone by the hotel staff. Markham was grateful for a little company, and fed his shrew on biscuits and dry bread. It moved about his room quite freely and slept in the bottom drawer of his dressing table. Unlike the cat, it had no objection to Markham's face or lack of it.

Towards the end of August, when there was still no relief from the endless rain and cloying mist, Markham grew restless again. He made one brief, nocturnal visit to the park behind the hotel, and came back soaked to the skin. It seemed a pointless exercise, tramping through the long, leech-infested grass. What he really longed for was to touch that piano again. Bits of old music ran through his head. He wanted to pick out a few tunes on that cracked old instrument in the deserted ballroom.

The rain was thundering down on the corrugated tin roofs. There had been a power failure—common enough on nights like this—and most of the town, including the hotel, had been plunged into darkness. There was no need of mask or cape. No need for his false nose, either. Only in the occasional flash of lightning could you see his torn and ravaged countenance.

Markham slipped out of his room and made his way through the cellars beneath the ballroom. It was a veritable jungle down there. No longer used as a wine cellar, the complex was really a storeroom for old and rotting furniture, rusty old boilers from another age, broken garden urns, even a chipped and mutilated statue of Cupid. It had stood in the garden in former times; but recently the town municipal committee had objected to it as being un-Indian and obscene and so it had been banished to the cellar.

That had been several years ago, and since then no one had been down into the cellars. It was Markham's short cut to the living world above.

It had stopped raining, and a sliver of moon shone through the clouds. There were still no lights in the hotel. But Markham was used to darkness. He slipped into the ballroom and approached the old piano.

He sat there for half an hour, strumming out old tunes.

There was one old favourite that kept coming back to him, and he played it again and again, recalling the words as he went along.

> *Oh, pale dispenser of my joys and pains,*
> *Holding the doors of Heaven and of Hell,*
> *How the hot blood rushed wildly through the*
> *veins*
> *Beneath your touch, until you waved farewell.*

The words of Laurence Hope's *Kashmiri Love Song* took him back to happier times when life seemed full of possibilities. And when he came to the end of the song, he felt his loss even more passionately:

> *Pale hands, pink-tipped, like lotus buds that float*
> *On these cool waters where we used to dwell,*
> *I would rather have felt you round my throat*
> *crushing out life, than waving me farewell!*

He had loved and been loved once. But that had been a long, long time ago. Pale hands he'd loved, beside the Shalimar . . .

He stopped playing. All was still.

Should he return to his room now, and keep his promise to Negi? But then again no one was likely to be around on a night like this, reasoned Markham; and he had no intention of entering any of the rooms. Through the glass doors at the other end of the ballroom he could see a faint glow, as of a firefly in the darkness. He moved towards the light, as a moth to a flame. It was the chowkidar's lantern. He lay asleep on an old sofa, from which the stuffing was protruding.

Markham's was a normal mind handicapped by a physical abnormality. But how long can a mind remain normal in such circumstances?

Markham took the chowkidar's lamp and advanced into the lobby. Moth-eaten stags' heads stared down at him from the walls. They had been shot about a hundred years ago, when the hunting of animals had been in fashion. The taxidermist's art had given them a semblance of their former nobility; but time had taken its toll. A mounted panther's head had lost its glass eyes. Even so, thought Markham wryly, its head is in better shape than mine!

The door of the barroom opened to a gentle pressure. The bartender had been tippling on the quiet and had neglected to close the door properly. Markham placed the lamp on a table and looked up at the bottles arrayed in front of him. Some foreign wines, sherries and vermouth. Rum, gin and vodka. He'd never been much of a drinker; drink went to his head rather too quickly, he'd always know that. But the bottles certainly looked attractive, and he felt in need of some sustenance, so he poured himself a generous peg of whisky and drank it neat. A warm glow spread through his body. He felt a little better about himself. Life could be made tolerable if he had more frequent access to the bar!

Pacing about in her room on the floor above, Mrs Khanna heard a noise downstairs. She had always suspected the bartender, Ram Lal, of helping himself to liquor on the quiet. After ten o'clock, his gait was unsteady, and in the mornings he often turned up rather groggy and unshaven. Well, she was going to catch him red-handed tonight!

Markham sat on a bar-stool with his back to the swing doors. Mrs Khanna, entering on tiptoe, could only make out the outline of a man's figure pouring himself a drink.

The wind in the passage muffled the sound of Mrs Khanna's approach. And anyway, Markham's mind was far away, in the distant Shalimar Bagh where hands, pink-tipped, touched his lips and cheeks, his face yet undespoiled.

'Ram Lal!' hissed Mrs Khanna, intent on scaring the bartender out of his wits. 'Having a good time again?'

Markham was startled, but he did not lose his head. He did not turn immediately.

'I'm not Ram Lal, Mrs Khanna,' said Markham quietly. 'Just one of your guests. An old resident, in fact. You've seen me around before. My face was badly injured a long time ago. I'm not very nice to look at. But there's nothing to be afraid of. I'm quite normal, you know.'

Markham got up slowly. He held his cape up to his face and began moving slowly towards the swing doors. But Mrs Khanna was having none of it. She reached out and snatched at the cape. In the flickering lamplight she stared into that dreadful face. She opened her mouth to scream.

But Markham did not want to hear her screams again. They shattered the stillness and beauty of the night. There was nothing beautiful about a woman's screams—especially Mrs Khanna's.

He reached out for his tormentor and grabbed her by the throat. He wanted to stop her screaming, that was all. But he had strong hands. Struggling, the pair of them knocked over a chair and fell against the table.

'Quite normal, Mrs Khanna,' he said, again and again, his voice ascending. 'I'm quite normal!'

Her legs slid down beneath a bar stool. Still he held on, squeezing, pressing. All those years of frustration were in that grip. Crushing out life and waving it farewell!

Involuntarily, she flung out an arm and knocked over the lamp. Markham released his grip; she fell heavily to the carpet. A rivulet of burning oil sped across the floor and set fire to the hem of her nightgown. But Mrs Khanna was now oblivious to what was happening. The flames took hold of a curtain and ran up towards the wooden ceiling.

Markham picked up a jug of water and threw it on the flames. It made no difference. Horrified, he dashed through the swing doors and called for help. The chowkidar stirred sluggishly and called out: 'Khabardar! Who goes there?' He saw a red glow in the bar, rubbed his eyes in consternation, and began looking for his lamp. He did not really need one. Bright flames were leaping out of the French windows.

'Fire!' shouted the chowkidar, and ran for help.

The old hotel, with its timbered floors and ceilings, oaken beams and staircases, mahogany and rosewood furniture, was a veritable tinderbox. By the time the chowkidar could summon help, the fire had spread to the dining room and was licking its way up the stairs to the first-floor rooms.

Markham had already ascended the staircase and was pounding on doors, shouting, 'Get up, get up! Fire below!' He ran to the far end of the corridor, where Negi had his room, and pounded on the door with his fists until Negi woke up.

'The hotel's on fire!' shouted Markham, and ran back the way he had come. There was little more that he could do.

Some of the hotel staff were now rushing about with buckets of water, but the stairs and landing were ablaze, and those living on the first floor had to retreat to the servants' entrance, where a flight of stone steps led down to the tennis courts. Here they gathered, looking on in awe and consternation as the fire spread rapidly through the main building, showing itself at the windows as it went along. The small group on the tennis courts was soon joined by outsiders, for bad news spreads as fast as a good fire, and the townsfolk were not long in turning up.

Markham emerged on the roof, and stood there for some time, while the fire ran through the Empire Hotel, crackling vigorously and lighting up the sky. The people below spotted him on the roof, and waved and shouted to him to come down. Smoke billowed around him, and then he disappeared from view.

*

It was a fire to remember. The town hadn't seen anything like it since the Abbey School had gone up in flames forty years earlier, and only the older residents could remember that one. Negi and the hotel staff could only watch helplessly, as the fire raged through the old timbered building, consuming all that stood in its way. Everyone was out of the building, except Mrs Khanna, and as yet no one had any idea as to what had happened to her.

Towards morning it began raining heavily again, and this finally quenched the fire; but by then the buildings had been gutted, and the Empire Hotel, that had stood protectively over the town for over a hundred years, was no more.

Mrs Khanna's charred body was recovered from the ruins. A telegram was sent to Mr Khanna in Geneva, and phone calls were made to sundry relatives and insurance offices. Negi was very much in charge.

When the initial confusion was over, Negi remembered Markham and walked around to the rear of the gutted building and down the cellar steps. The basement and the cellar had escaped the worst of the fire, but they were still full of smoke. Negi found Markham's door open.

Markham was stretched out on his bed. The empty bottle of sleeping tablets on the bedside table told its own story; but it was more likely that he had suffocated from the smoke.

Markham's artificial nose lay on the dressing-table. Negi picked it up and placed it on the dead man's poor face.

The hotel had gone, and with it Negi's livelihood. An old friend had gone, too. An era had passed. But Negi was the sort who liked to tidy up afterwards.

The Garden of Memories

Sitting in the sun on a winter's afternoon, feeling my age just a little (I'm sixty-seven now), I began reminiscing about my boyhood in the Dehra of long ago, and I found myself missing the old times—friends of my youth, my grandmother, our neighbours, interesting characters in our small town, and, of course, my eccentric relative—the dashing young Uncle Ken!

Yes, Dehra was a small town then—uncluttered, uncrowded, with quiet lanes and pretty gardens and shady orchards.

The only time in my life that I was fortunate enough to live in a house with a real garden—as opposed to a back yard or balcony or windswept veranda—was during those three years when I spent my winter holidays (December to March) in Granny's bungalow on the Old Survey Road.

The best months were February and March, when the garden was heavy with the scent of sweet peas, the flower beds a many-coloured quilt of phlox, antirrhinum, larkspur, petunia and Californian poppy. I loved the bright yellows of the Californian poppies, the soft pinks of our own Indian poppies, the subtle perfume of petunias and snapdragons, and above all, the delicious, overpowering scent of the massed sweet peas which grew taller than me. Flowers made a sensualist of me. They taught me the delight of smell and colour and touch—yes, touch too, for to press a rose to one's lips is very like a gentle, hesitant, exploratory kiss . . .

Granny decided on what flowers should be sown, and where. Dhuki, the gardener, did the digging and weeding, sowing and transplanting. He was a skinny, taciturn old man, who had begun to resemble the weeds he flung away. He did not mind answering my questions, but never did he allow our brief conversations to interfere with his work. Most of the time he was to be found on his haunches, hoeing and weeding with a little spade called a 'khurpi'. He would throw out the smaller marigolds because he said Granny did not care for them. I felt sorry for these colourful little discards, collected them, and transplanted them to a little garden patch of my own at the back of the house, near the garden wall.

Another so-called weed that I liked was a little purple flower that grew in clusters all over Dehra, on any bit of wasteland, in ditches, on canal banks. It flowered from late winter into early summer, and it will be growing in the valley and beyond long after gardens have become obsolete, as indeed they must, considering the rapid spread of urban clutter. It brightens up fields and roads where you least expect a little colour. I have since learnt that it is called

Ageratum, and that it is actually prized as a garden flower in Europe, where it is described as 'Blue Mink' in the seed catalogues. Here it isn't blue but purple and it grows all the way from Rajpur (just above Dehra) to the outskirts of Meerut; then it disappears.

Other garden outcasts include the lantana bush, an attractive wayside shrub; the thorn apple, various thistles, daisies and dandelions. But both Granny and Dhuki had declared a war on weeds, and many of these commoners had to exist outside the confines of the garden. Like slum children, they survived rather well in ditches and on the roadside, while their more pampered fellow citizens were prone to leaf diseases and parasitic infections of various kinds.

The veranda was a place where Granny herself could potter about, attending to various ferns, potted palms and colourful geraniums. She averred that geraniums kept snakes away, although she never said why. As far as I know, snakes don't have a great sense of smell.

One day I saw a snake curled up at the bottom of the veranda steps. When it saw me, or became aware of my footsteps, it uncoiled itself and slithered away. I told Granny about it, and observed that it did not seem to be bothered by the geraniums.

'Ah,' said Granny. 'But for those geraniums, the snake would have entered the house!' There was no arguing with Granny.

Or with Uncle Ken, when he was at his most pontifical.

One day, while walking near the canal bank, we came upon a green grass snake holding a frog in its mouth. The frog was half in, half out, and with the help of my hockey stick, I made the snake disgorge the unfortunate creature. It hopped away, none the worse for its adventure.

I felt quite pleased with myself. 'Is this what it feels like to be God?' I mused aloud.

'No,' said Uncle Ken. 'God would have let the snake finish its lunch.'

Uncle Ken was one of those people who went through life without having to do much, although a great deal seemed to happen around him. He acted as a sort of catalyst for events that involved the family, friends, neighbours, the town itself. He believed in the fruits of hard work: other people's hard work.

Ken was good-looking as a boy, and his sisters doted on him. He took full advantage of their devotion, and, as the girls grew up and married, Ken took it for granted that they and their husbands would continue to look after his welfare. You could say he was the originator of the welfare state; his own.

I'll say this for Uncle Ken, he had a large fund of curiosity in his nature, and he loved to explore the town we lived in, and any other town or city where he might happen to find himself. With one sister settled in Lucknow, another in Ranchi, a third in Bhopal, a fourth in Pondicherry, and a fifth in Barrackpore, Uncle Ken managed to see a cross-section of India by dividing his time between all his sisters and their long-suffering husbands.

Uncle Ken liked to walk. Occasionally he borrowed my bicycle, but he had a tendency to veer off the main road and into ditches and other obstacles after a collision with a bullock cart, in which he tore his trousers and damaged the handlebar of my bicycle, Uncle Ken concluded that walking was the best way of getting around Dehra.

Uncle Ken dressed quite smartly for a man of no particular occupation. He had a blue-striped blazer and a red-striped blazer; he usually wore white or off-white trousers, immaculately pressed (by Granny). He was the delight of shoeshine boys, for he was always having his shoes polished. Summers he wore a straw hat, telling everyone he had worn it for the Varsity Boat Race, while rowing for Oxford (he hadn't been to England, let alone Oxford); winters, he wore one of Grandfather's old felt hats. He seldom went bareheaded. At thirty he was almost completely bald, prompting Aunt Mabel to remark: 'Well, Ken, you must be grateful for small mercies. At least you'll never have bats getting entangled in your hair.'

Thanks to all his walking Uncle Ken had a good digestion, which kept pace with a hearty appetite. Our walks would be punctuated by short stops at chaat shops, sweet shops, fruit stalls, confectioners, small bakeries and other eateries.

'Have you brought any pocket money along?' he would ask, for he was usually broke.

'Granny gave me five rupees.'

'We'll try some rasgullas, then.'

And the rasgullas would be followed by gulab jamuns until my five rupees was finished. Uncle Ken received a small allowance from Granny, but he ferreted it away to spend on clothes, preferring to spend my pocket money on perishables such as ice creams, kulfis and Indian sweets.

On one occasion, when neither of us had any money, Uncle Ken decided to venture into a sugarcane field on the outskirts of the town. He had broken off a stick of cane, and was busy chewing on it, when the owner of the field spotted us and let out a volley of imprecations. We fled from the field with the irate farmer giving chase. I could run faster than Uncle Ken, and did so. The farmer would have caught up with Uncle Ken if the latter's hat hadn't blown off, causing a diversion. The farmer picked up the hat, examined it, seemed to fancy it, and put it on. Several small boys clapped and cheered. The farmer marched off, wearing the hat, and Uncle Ken wisely decided against making any attempt to retrieve it.

'I'll get another one,' he said philosophically.

He wore a pith helmet, or sola topee, for the next few days, as he thought it would protect him from sticks and stones. For a while he harboured a paranoia that all the sugarcane farmers in the valley were looking for him, to avenge his foray into their fields. But after some time he discarded the topee because, according to him, it interfered with his good looks.

*

Granny grew the best sweet peas in Dehra. But she never entered them at the Annual Flower Show, held every year in the second week of March. She did not grow flowers to win prizes, she said; she grew them to please the spirit of Grandfather, who still hovered about the house and grounds he'd built thirty years earlier.

Miss Kellner, Granny's crippled but valued tenant, said the flowers were grown to attract beautiful butterflies, and she was right. In early summer, swarms of butterflies flitted about the garden.

Uncle Ken had no compunction about winning prizes, even though he did nothing to deserve them. Without telling anyone, he submitted a large display of Granny's sweet peas for the flower show, and when the prizes were announced, lo and behold! Kenneth Clerke had been awarded first prize for his magnificent display of sweet peas.

Granny refused to speak to him for several days.

Uncle Ken had been hoping for a cash prize, but they gave him a flower vase. He told me it was a Ming vase. But it looked more like Meerut to me. He offered it to Granny, hoping to propitiate her; but, still displeased with him, she gave it to Mr Khastgir, the artist next door, who kept his paintbrushes in it.

Although I was sometimes a stubborn and unruly boy (my hero was Richmal Crompton's 'William'), I got on well with old ladies, especially those who, like Miss Kellner, were fond of offering me chocolates, marzipans, soft nankattai biscuits (made at Yusuf's bakery in the Dilaram Bazaar), and pieces of crystallized ginger. Miss Kellner couldn't walk—had never walked—and so she could only admire the garden from a distance, but it was from her that I learnt the names of many flowers, trees, birds and even butterflies.

Uncle Ken wasn't any good at names, but he wanted to catch a rare butterfly. He said he could make a fortune if he caught a leaf butterfly called the Purple Emperor. He equipped himself with a butterfly net, a bottle of ether, and a cabinet for mounting his trophies; he then prowled all over the grounds, making frequent forays at anything that flew. He caught several common species—Red Admirals, a

Tortoiseshell, a Painted Lady, even the occasional dragonfly—but the high-flying Purple Emperor and other exotics eluded him, as did the fortune he was always aspiring to make.

Eventually he caught an angry wasp, which stung him through the netting. Chased by its fellow wasps, he took refuge in the lily pond and emerged sometime later draped in lilies and water weeds.

After this, Uncle Ken retired from the butterfly business, insisting that tiger-hunting was safer.

The Ghost in the Garden

Behind the house there was an orchard where guava, lichee and papaya trees mingled with two or three tall mango trees. The guava trees were easy to climb. The lichee trees gave a lot of shade—as well as bunches of delicious lichees in the summer. The mango trees were at their most attractive in the spring, when their blossoms gave out a heady fragrance.

But there was one old mango tree, near the boundary wall, where no one, not even Dhuki the gardener, ever went.

'It doesn't give any fruit,' said Dhuki, when I questioned him. 'It's an old tree.'

'Then why don't we cut it down?'

'We will, one day, when your grandmother wishes. . .'

The weeds grew thick in that corner of the garden. They were safe there from Dhuki's relentless weeding.

'Why doesn't anyone go to that corner of the orchard ?' I asked Miss Kellner, our crippled tenant, who had been in Dehra since she was a girl.

But she didn't want to talk about it. Uncle Ken, too, changed the subject whenever I brought it up.

So I wandered about the orchard on my own, cautiously making my way towards that neglected and forbidden corner of the garden until Dhuki called me back.

'Don't go there, *baba*,' he cautioned. 'It's unlucky.'

'Why doesn't anyone go near the old mango tree?' I asked Granny.

She just shook her head and turned away. There was obviously something that no one wanted me to know. So I disobeyed and ignored everyone, and in the still of the afternoon, when most of the household was taking a siesta, I walked over to the old mango tree at the end of the garden.

It was a cool, shady place, and seemed friendly enough. But there were no birds in the tree; no squirrels, either. And this was unusual. I sat down on the grass, with my back against the trunk of the tree, and peered out at the sunlit house and garden. In the shimmering heat haze I thought I saw someone walking through the trees, but it wasn't Dhuki or anyone I knew.

It had been a hot day, but presently I began to feel cold; and then I found myself shivering, as though a fever had suddenly come on. I looked up into the tree, and the branch above me was moving, swaying slightly, although there was no breeze and all the other leaves and branches were still.

I felt I had to get out of the cold, but I found it difficult to get up. So I crawled across the grass on my hands and knees, until I was in the bright sunlight. The shivering

29

passed and I ran across to the house and did not look back at the mango tree until I had reached the verandah.

I told Miss Kellner about my experience.

'Were you frightened?' she asked.

'Yes—a little,' I confessed.

'And did you see anything?'

'Some of the branches moved—I felt very cold—but there was no wind.'

'Did you hear anything?'

'Just a soft moaning sound.'

'It's an old tree. It groans when it feels its age—just as I do!'

I did not go near the mango tree for some time, and I did not mention the incident to Granny or Uncle Ken. I had by now realized that the subject was taboo with them.

*

As a boy I was always exploring lonely places—neglected gardens and orchards, unoccupied houses, patches of scrub or wasteland, the fields outside the town, the fringes of the forest. On one of my rambles behind the bungalow, I pushed my way through a thicket of lantana bushes and stumbled over a thick stone slab, twisting my ankle slightly as I fell. For some time I sat on the grass massaging my foot. When the pain eased, I looked more closely at the stone slab and was surprised to find that it was a gravestone. It was almost entirely covered by ivy; obviously no one had been near it for years. I tugged at the ivy and some of it came away in my hands. There was some indistinct lettering on the grave, half-obscured by grass and moss. I could make out a name—Rose—but little more.

I sat there for some time, pondering over my discovery, and wondering why 'Rose' should have been buried at so lonely a spot when there was a cemetery not far away. Why hadn't she been interred beside her kith and kind? Had she wished it so? And why?

Only Miss Kellner seemed willing to answer my questions, and it was to her I went, where she sat in her armchair under the pomalo tree—the armchair from which she never moved except when she was carried bodily to her bed or bathroom by the ayah or a couple of her rickshaw boys. I can never forget crippled Miss Kellner in her armchair in the garden, playing patience with a well-worn pack of cards—and always patient with me whenever I interrupted her game with endless questions about neighbours or relatives or her own history. Even as a boy, the past fascinated me. I don't mean the history of nations; I mean individual histories, the way people lived, and why they were happy or unhappy, and why they sometimes did terrible things for no apparent rhyme or reason.

'Miss Kellner,' I asked, 'whose grave is that in the jungle behind the house?'

She looked at me over the rim of her pince-nez. 'How would you expect me to know, child? Do I look as though I could climb walls, looking for old graves? Have you asked your grandmother?'

'Granny won't tell me anything. And Uncle Ken pretends to know everything when he knows nothing.'

'So how should I know?'

'You've been here a long time.'

'Only twenty years. That happened before I came to this house.'

'*What* happened?'

'Oh, you are a trying boy. Why must you know everything?'

'It's better than *not* knowing.'

'Are you sure? Sometimes it's better not to know.'

'Sometimes, maybe . . . But I *like* to know. Who was Rose?'

'Your grandfather's first wife.'

'Oh.' This came as a surprise. I hadn't heard about grandfather's first marriage. 'But why is she buried in such a lonely place? Why not in the cemetery?'

'Because she took her own life. And in those days a suicide couldn't be given Christian burial in a cemetery. Now is your curiosity satisfied?'

But my appetite had only been whetted for more information. 'And why did she commit suicide?'

'I really don't know, child. Why would anyone? Because they are unhappy, tired of living, in distress over something or the other.'

'You're not tired of living, are you? Even though you can't walk and your fingers are all crooked . . .'

'Don't be rude, or you won't find any meringues in my pantry! My fingers are good enough for writing, and for poking small boys in the ribs.' And she gave me a sharp poke which made me yelp. 'No, I'm not tired of life—not yet—but people are made differently, you know. And your grandfather isn't around to tell us what happened. And of course he married again—your grandmother . . .'

'Would *she* have known the first one?'

'I don't think so. She met your grandfather much later. But she doesn't like to talk about these things.'

'And how did Rose commit suicide?'

'I have no idea.'

'Of course you know, Miss Kellner. You can't bluff me. You know everything!'

'I wasn't here, I tell you.'

'But you heard all about it. And *I* know how she did it. She must have hanged herself from that mango tree—the tree at the end of the garden, which everyone avoids. I told you I went there one day, and it was very cold and lonely in its shade. I was frightened, you know.'

'Yes,' said Miss Kellner pensively. 'She must have been lonely, poor thing. She wasn't very stable, I'm told. Used to wander about on her own, picking wildflowers, singing to herself, sometimes getting lost and coming home at odd hours. How does the old song go? 'Lonely as the desert breeze . . .' In her croaky voice, Miss Kellner sang a refrain from an old ballad, before continuing, 'Your grandfather was very fond of her. He wasn't a cruel man. He put up with her strange ways. But sometimes he lost patience and scolded her and once or twice had even to lock her up. *That* was frightening, because then she would start screaming. It was a mistake locking her up. Never lock anyone up, child . . . Something seemed to snap inside her. She became violent at times.'

'How do you know all this, Miss Kellner?'

'Your grandfather would sometimes come over and tell me his troubles. I was living in another house then, a little way down the road. Poor man, he had a trying time with Rose. He was thinking of sending her to Ranchi, to the mental hospital. Then, early one morning, he found her hanging from the mango tree. Her spirit had flown away, like the bluebird she always wanted to be.'

After that, I did not go near the old mango tree; I found it rather menacing, as though it had actually participated in that dark deed . . . Poor innocent tree, being saddled with the emotions of unbalanced humans! But I did visit the neglected grave and cleaned the weeds away, so that the inscription came out more clearly: 'Rose, dearly beloved wife of Henry—(my maternal grandfather's surname followed). And when Dhuki wasn't looking, I plucked a red rose from the garden and placed it on the grave.

One afternoon, when Granny was at a bridge-party and Uncle Ken was taking a walk, I rummaged through the storeroom adjoining the back veranda, leafing through old scrapbooks and magazines. Behind a pile of books I discovered an old wind-up gramophone, an album of well-preserved gramophone records, and a box of steel needles. I took the gramophone into the sitting-room and tried out one of the records. It sounded all right. So I played a few more. They were all songs of yesteryear, romantic ballads sung by tenors and baritones who were popular in the 1920s and 30s. Granny did not listen to music, and the gramophone had been neglected a long time. Now, for the first time in many years, the room was full of melody. *One Alone, I'll See You Again, Will You Remember?, Only A Rose . . .*

Only a rose
to give you,
Only a song

dying away,
Only a smile
to keep in memory

It was while this tender love song was playing that a transformation seemed to come over the room.

At first it grew darker. Then a soft pink glow suffused the room, and I saw the figure of a woman, a smiling melancholy woman in white, drifting, rather than walking, towards me. She stopped in the centre of the room, and appeared to be watching me. She wore the long flowing dress of an earlier day, and her hair was arranged in a sort of coiffure that I'd seen in old photographs.

As the song came to an end, the apparition vanished. The room was normal again. I put away the gramophone and the records. I felt disturbed rather than afraid, and I did not wish to conjure up further emanations from the past.

But in my dreams that night I saw the beautiful sad lady again. She was waltzing in the garden, sometimes by herself, sometimes partnered by other phantom dancers. She beckoned to me in my dream, inviting me to join her, but I remained standing on the veranda steps until she danced away into the distance and faded from view.

And in the morning when I woke I found a red rose, moist with dew, lying beside my pillow.

Return of the White Pigeon

About fifty years ago, on the outskirts of Dehra Dun, there lived a happily married couple, an English colonel and his beautiful Persian wife. They were both enthusiastic gardeners, and their beautiful bungalow was covered with bougainvillaea and *Gul-i-Phanoos*, while in the garden the fragrance of the rose challenged the sweet scent of the jasmine.

They had lived together many years when the wife suddenly became very ill. Nothing could be done for her. As she lay dying, she told her servants that she would return to her beloved garden in the form of a white pigeon so that she could be near her husband and the place she loved so dearly.

The couple had no children, and as the years passed after his wife's death the Colonel found life very lonely. When he met an attractive English widow a few years younger than himself, he married her and brought her home to his beautiful house. But as he was carrying his new bride through the porch and up the veranda steps, a white pigeon came fluttering into the garden and perched on a rose bush. There it remained for a long time, cooing and murmuring in a sad, subdued manner.

Every day it entered the garden and alighted on the rose bush where it would call sadly and persistently. The servants became upset and even frightened. They remembered their previous mistress's dying promise, and they were convinced that her spirit dwelt in the white pigeon.

When the Colonel's new wife heard the story, she was naturally upset. Her husband did not give any credence to the tale, but when he saw how troubled his wife looked, he decided to do something about it. And so one day, when the pigeon appeared, he took his rifle and slipped out of the house, quietly making his way down the verandah steps. When he saw the pigeon on the rose bush, he raised his gun, took aim, and fired.

There was a high-pitched woman's scream. And then the pigeon flew away unsteadily, its white breast dark with blood. Where it fell, no one knew.

That same night the Colonel died in his sleep. The doctor put it down to heart failure, which was true enough; but the servants said he had always kept good health, and they were sure his death had something to do with the killing of the white pigeon.

The Colonel's widow left Dehra Dun, and the beautiful bungalow fell into ruin. The garden became a jungle, and jackals passed through the abandoned rooms. The Colonel had been buried in the grounds of his estate, and the gravestone can still be found, although the inscription has long since disappeared.

Few people pass that way. But those who do, say that they have often seen a white pigeon resting on the grave; a white pigeon with a crimson stain on its breast.

Young Man in a Tonga

Ever since I was five, tongas and their drivers have been great favourites with me. I do not count the tonga-driver who eloped with my beloved ayah. Though I could not help admiring his bright green waistcoat and the swiftness of his pony, I could never forgive him for stealing the heart of my ayah, a heart which had, till then, been entirely in my possession. His elopement left me with a vague prejudice against tonga-drivers—until I met Latif.

Latif was a dreamy sort of fellow who should have been writing poetry instead of driving a two-wheeled buggy for a living. He did occasionally dabble in verse, whenever he could find a sufficient amount of inspiration in women or alcohol. He was, by his own account, descended from one of the Nawabs of Avadh, and he kept his glossy black hair at shoulder-length in order to look the part of a decadent poet-nawab.

He was slim, wore the cool, airy Lucknow kurta and pyjama, and outlined his eyes with kohl.

I must have been seven years old when I first met him. It was raining heavily. I had hoped that this would prevent me from attending school, but my grandmother, with whom I was frequently at war, sent the servant out for a tonga.

It came rattling up the driveway, the pony splashing through the puddles, the wheels churning up soft mud. The driver salaamed, and I clambered up on the front seat beside him. I had decided that I would at least enjoy the ride to school; and that could only be done by sitting in the front seat.

Away we went.

That first ride with Latif made me his devoted admirer. The rain, and the wind whipping it across our faces, seemed to unleash the high spirits of both Latif and his pony. Shouting profanities and endearments at the beast, he sent the tonga careering along the road at break-neck speed.

He gave me a sly look out of the corner of his eyes to see how I was reacting to this mad, Gilpin-like gallop; and when he saw that I was enjoying it (though a trifle apprehensively), he drew me nearer and, making his whip sing through the air and twang on his pony's rump, he had us going at such a spanking pace that my school was left far behind before I realized we had passed it.

But we had made such good time that I wasn't late. When he put me down at the school gate, he said, 'My name is Latif. Whenever you want a tonga ride, send for me, all right? Are we friends?'

'Certainly,' I said. 'And when I grow up, I will have a tonga like yours.'

He laughed at that—afterwards I thought it might have been a slightly bitter laugh—and sent his pony cantering down the road, while I gazed after the contraption with worshipful admiration.

As it was the monsoon season, we had many rides together; sometimes to and from school, and sometimes even further afield, off the main road, across the little river bed, through fields and a small village, and then home by a short cut through the slums of the town.

When I was sent to a boarding school in the hills, I deeply missed Latif and his tonga. It was not only the rides that I missed, but the man himself, his lively conversation, sly grin, the Urdu poetry which he recited aloud and which I was never able to follow, the songs he shouted at the top of his voice.

I would, of course, come down to the plains for my winter holidays, and Latif would always be there, his tonga bells jingling at the gate. He would look thinner and a little wilder each year, but never older. I never did know how old he was. There is something deceptive in the appearance of a person suffering from tuberculosis, and Latif's youth and high spirits were all the more noticeable for their impermanence. The tendency to snatch at life, to sweep together greedily all the sensations life offers, is said to be characteristic of the consumptive temperament.

Tongas were no longer a common sight in the town. Buses and cycle-rickshaws were beginning to take their place. But Latif wasn't strong enough to pedal a cycle-rickshaw all day in the heat, and he persevered with his tonga in spite of diminishing returns. I don't think he would have given it up even if he could have run a rickshaw or driven a bus.

He did not eat much but he kept himself going on some orange-coloured country liquor. Whether this stuff shortened his life or helped to extend it, I couldn't say. But it helped him to laugh at his poverty, and to recite new verses, and to gallop his pony even faster—and that, of course, was what I wanted.

I was fifteen when we had our most daring adventure.

Latif overtook me in the evening while I was walking home from a cinema. At first he set his pony's head in the direction of my house; then he suggested a brief spin on the outskirts of the town. As it was not yet dark, I readily agreed. He gave a shout of joy, promised his pony all the pleasures of the bridal bed, and sent the ageing creature cantering through the mango groves that surrounded the town.

We were soon in the countryside, and Latif would every now and then reach down under the seat where fodder was kept, produce a large bottle of orange liquor and take a generous swig from it. I, too, occasionally put the bottle to my lips, but it was like an acid tearing at the walls of my stomach and I gladly handed my companion the lion's share.

It had grown dark, and I suggested that we return home. Latif, always ready to oblige, turned the tonga about. It may have been the darkness, or the drink, but he took the pony down an altogether different road which grew narrower and more bumpy as we went along. Finally, the pony blew hard through its nostrils and came to a halt.

The reins slipped from Latif's fingers, he slid his length along the seat and broke into loud snoring.

Knowing that I ought to have been at home long before this, I was far from sleepy. I got down from the tonga and tramped back along the broken path until I reached the main road. There I waited until a bullock cart came along. Begging a ride, I got back to town and finally reached home at about ten o'clock. My grandmother was furious, but she finally believed my story that the film was *Gone with the Wind* and that it had lasted almost four hours.

To this day I don't know how Latif got home. Perhaps he spent the night in the open, in his tonga. When I met him a few weeks later, he did not remember the incident! He was looking pale and rather emaciated; and he told me he had been sick.

'It's this cough of mine,' he complained. 'My friend, I am coughing my lifeblood away. One of these days I will simply fade into invisibility, and the world will have lost a great poet.' Then, seeing that I was not very impressed, he added, 'And you will have lost a great tonga-driver.'

He was right, of course. He had no equal when it came to dealing with tongas. But he was no longer a common sight on the roads. His beautiful hair had lost much of its sheen, and his eyes, always bright, looked brighter than ever in his cavernous face.

But he still laughed at himself and at the world, and continued to compose his verses. His poetry was spontaneous, arising from the immediate moment, and as he never put any of it down on paper—he was much too lazy—it has been lost to posterity.

One evening I saw his tonga standing by itself under a tall peepul tree, and I called out, 'Latif, will you take me home today?'

The man who looked up at me from the other side of the carriage was not Latif, but a rather coarse-looking individual with paan-stained teeth. But I could not mistake the pony and the tonga.

'Where is Latif?' I asked.

'Gone,' said the stranger.

'Gone where?'

'God knows. But that he has gone a considerable distance I am absolutely certain, because I helped to bury him last week. He coughed his lungs out one night, and there was very little left of him to bury. His wife and children sold me this tonga of his, so they have enough to carry on with for a few months.'

I had not known that Latif possessed a wife and children in addition to his tonga. He had never told me anything about his private life, and I had never been curious. For me, he had been inseparable from his pony. He had been a wild, exulting fellow who liked the breeze slapping him in the face and the ground swerving and snaking beneath him, as he galloped through life with all the exhilaration of the short-lived.

I vowed that I would allow no other tonga-driver to replace Latif in my life and affections. And I sent up a prayer, to his God and mine and whatever gods there be, that my friend might find large numbers of fast ponies wherever they chose to send him.

The Writer's Bar

For some time now, Nandu has had this notion, or dream if you like, of naming the old Savoy bar the 'Writers' Bar'.

'But to do that,' I said, 'You'd have to get a few writers in here, wouldn't you?'

'Well, you're one, aren't you? Don't you have any writer friends?'

'Hardly any. And the few I know are teetotallers. The Hemingway type is out of fashion.'

'Last year, when I was in Singapore,' said Nandu, 'I revisited the historic Raffles Hotel—it's about the same age as the Savoy—and they had a Writer's Bar with brass plaques on the walls stating that Somerset Maugham had been there, and Joseph Conrad, and Graham Greene.'

'All very sober people,' I remarked.

'Yes, but they stayed there, and they must have had the occasional drink at the Bar, even if it was only a nimbu pani.'

'Well, in the good old days, the Savoy must have had the occasional writer staying here.'

'There was Pearl Buck. I still have her autograph in one of her books. She won the Nobel Prize, didn't she?'

'She did, but I doubt if she frequented the bar. I believe she was the daughter of missionaries.'

'All the more reason for taking to drink. In any case, she must have looked in here from time to time. We'll put her name on a plaque.'

'All right. We've got Pearl Buck.'

'What about Rudyard Kipling? He must have stayed here.'

'My dear chap,' I said. 'The hotel opened in 1905. By that time Kipling had left India, never to return.'

'You're not being very helpful,' said Nandu. 'What about John Masters?'

'Quite possible,' I said. 'He served with a Gurkha regiment in Dehra Dun. Must have come up the hill occasionally. Probably dropped in for a drink. Here or at the Charleville.'

'Forget about the Charleville, it burnt down years ago. We'll give John Masters a plaque. That's two we've got!'

'Why don't we look up the old hotel register?' I asked.

'The previous manager walked off with it,' said Nandu ruefully.

'Probably wanted Pearl Buck's autograph.'

'Who was that fellow who wrote about the separation bell? You know, the bell they used to ring at four every morning so that people could get back to their own rooms?'

'I've heard of the bell,' I said. 'But I can't remember the name of the writer.'

'Somerset Maugham?'

'I don't think he visited Mussoorie. It was a travel writer.'

'The Gantzers? Bill Aitken?'

'They are still alive. But if you ask them in for a drink, they might let you put their names up.'

'A free drink, you mean?' Nandu didn't look too happy.

'Naturally.'

'Let's stick to the dead. Pandit Nehru stayed here. He was a writer.'

'Yes, Nandu. But I don't think you'd have found him in the bar.'

'Sir Edmund Hillary?'

'Well, he wrote his autobiography. Probably stopped by for a drink after climbing Everest.'

'All right, I've got it! Jim Corbett!'

'But he lived in Naini Tal,' I protested. 'I doubt if he ever came here.'

'His parents were married in Mussoorie. You told me so yourself. And he wrote that book, *The Maneater of Rudraprayag.* Rudraprayag is only eighty miles from here, as the crow flies.'

'All right, all right. And after shooting the maneater, Corbett tramped all the way to Mussoorie to have a refreshing beer at the Savoy. There was no motor road then, Nandu. He must have needed a drink very badly.'

'It's possible. He used to walk great distances.'

'To shoot maneaters, not to drink beer. But let's give him a plaque, on the strength of his parents having been married in Mussoorie. Who do we have now?'

'Pearl Buck, John Masters, Jim Corbett!'

The plaques are being prepared. The Writers' Bar will be inaugurated in the spring. If any reader can come up with a suitable candidate for inclusion, he'll be entitled to a free drink.

Only the other evening, when I was into my third whisky, a gentleman who looked exactly like Rudyard Kipling, walked up to the bar and asked the barman, 'Do you serve spirits?'

Before we could ask him to join us, he'd vanished.

Topaz

It seemed strange to be listening to the strains of 'The Blue Danube' while gazing out at the pine-clad slopes of the Himalayas, worlds apart. And yet the music of the waltz seemed singularly appropriate. A light breeze hummed through the pines, and the branches seemed to move in time to the music. The record player was new, but the records were old, picked up in a junk shop behind the Mall.

Below the pines there were oaks, and one oak tree in particular caught my eye. It was the biggest of the lot and stood by itself on a little knoll below the cottage. The breeze was not strong enough to lift its heavy old branches, but something was moving, swinging gently from the tree, keeping time to the music of the waltz, dancing . . .

It was someone hanging from the tree.

A rope oscillated in the breeze, the body turned slowly, turned this way and that, and I saw the face of a girl, her hair hanging loose, her eyes sightless, hands and feet limp; just turning, turning, while the waltz played on.

I turned off the player and ran downstairs.

Down the path through the trees, and on to the grassy knoll where the big oak stood.

A long-tailed magpie took fright and flew out from the branches, swooping low across the ravine. In the tree there was no one, nothing. A great branch extended halfway across the knoll, and it was possible for me to reach up and touch it. A girl could not have reached it without climbing the tree.

As I stood there, gazing up into the branches, someone spoke behind me.

'What are you looking at?'

I swung round. A girl stood in the clearing, facing me, a girl of seventeen or eighteen; alive, healthy, with bright eyes and a tantalizing smile. She was lovely to look at. I hadn't seen such a pretty girl in years.

'You startled me,' 'I said. 'You came up so unexpectedly.'

'Did you see anything—in the tree?' she asked.

'I thought I saw someone from my window. That's why I came down. Did *you* see anything?'

'No.' She shook her head, the smile leaving her face for a moment. 'I don't see anything. But other people do—sometimes.'

'What do they see?'

'My sister.'

'Your *sister*?'

'Yes. She hanged herself from this tree. It was many years ago. But sometimes you can see her hanging there.'

She spoke matter-of-factly: whatever had happened seemed very remote to her.

We both moved some distance away from the tree. Above the knoll, on a disused private tennis court (a relic from the hill station's colonial past) was a small stone bench. She sat down on it, and, after a moment's hesitation, I sat down beside her.

'Do you live close by?' I asked.

'Further up the hill. My father has a small bakery.'

She told me her name—Hameeda. She had two younger brothers.

'You must have been quite small when your sister died.'

'Yes. But I remember her. She was pretty.'

'Like you.'

She laughed in disbelief. 'Oh, I am nothing compared to her. You should have seen my sister.'

'Why did she kill herself?'

'Because she did not want to live. That's the only reason, no? She was to have been married but she loved someone else, someone who was not of her own community. It's an old story and the end is always sad, isn't it?'

'Not always. But what happened to the boy—the one she loved? Did he kill himself too?'

'No, he took a job in some other place. Jobs are not easy to get, are they?'

'I don't know. I've never tried for one.'

'Then what do you do?'

'I write stories.'

'Do people *buy* stories?'

'Why not? If your father can sell bread, I can sell stories.'

'People must have bread. They can live without stories.'

'No, Hameeda, you're wrong. People can't live without stories.'

*

Hameeda! I couldn't help loving her. Just loving her. No fierce desire or passion had taken hold of me. It wasn't like that. I was happy just to look at her, watch her while she sat on the grass outside my cottage, her lips stained with the juice of wild bilberries. She chatted away—about her friends, her clothes, her favourite things.

'Won't your parents mind if you come here every day?' I asked.

'I have told them you are teaching me.'

'Teaching you what?'

'They did not ask. You can tell me stories.'

So I told her stories.

It was midsummer.

The sun glinted on the ring she wore on her third finger: a translucent golden topaz, set in silver.

'That's a pretty ring,' I remarked.

'You wear it,' she said, impulsively removing it from her hand. 'It will give you good thoughts. It will help you to write better stories.'

She slipped it on to my little finger.

'I'll wear it for a few days,' I said. 'Then you must let me give it back to you.'

On a day that promised rain I took the path down to the stream at the bottom of the hill. There I found

Hameeda gathering ferns from the shady places along the rocky ledges above the water.

'What will you do with them?' I asked.

'This is a special kind of fern. You can cook it as a vegetable.'

'It is tasty?'

'No, but it is good for rheumatism.'

'Do you suffer from rheumatism?'

'Of course not. They are for my grandmother, she is very old.'

'There are more ferns further upstream,' I said. 'But we'll have to get into the water.'

We removed our shoes and began paddling upstream. The ravine became shadier and narrower, until the sun was almost completely shut out. The ferns grew right down to the water's edge. We bent to pick them but instead found ourselves in each other's arms; and sank slowly, as in a dream, into the soft bed of ferns, while overhead a whistling thrush burst out in dark sweet song.

'It isn't time that's passing by,' it seemed to say. 'It is you and I. It is you and I . . .'

*

I waited for her the following day, but she did not come.

Several days passed without my seeing her.

Was she sick? Had she been kept at home? Had she been sent away? I did not even know where she lived, so I could not ask. And if I had been able to ask, what would I have said?

Then one day I saw a boy delivering bread and pastries at the little tea shop about a mile down the road. From the upward slant of his eyes, I caught a slight resemblance to Hameeda. As he left the shop, I followed him up the hill. When I came abreast of him, I asked: 'Do you have your own bakery?'

He nodded cheerfully, 'Yes. Do you want anything—bread, biscuits, cakes? I can bring them to your house.'

'Of course. But don't you have a sister? A girl called Hameeda?'

His expression changed. He was no longer friendly. He looked puzzled and slightly apprehensive.

'Why do you want to know?'

'I haven't seen her for some time.'

'We have not seen her either.'

'Do you mean she has gone away?'

'Didn't you know? You must have been away a long time. It is many years since she died. She killed herself. You did not hear about it?'

'But wasn't that her sister—your other sister?'

'I had only one sister—Hameeda—and she died, when I was very young. It's an old story, ask someone else about it.'

He turned away and quickened his pace, and I was left standing in the middle of the road, my head full of questions that couldn't be answered.

That night there was a thunderstorm. My bedroom window kept banging in the wind. I got up to close it and, as I looked out, there was a flash of lightning and I saw that frail body again, swinging from the oak tree.

I tried to make out the features, but the head hung down and the hair was blowing in the wind.

Was it all a dream?'

It was impossible to say. But the topaz on my hand glowed softly in the darkness. And a whisper from the forest seemed to say, 'It isn't time that's passing by, my friend. It is you and I . . .'

Susanna's Seven Husbands

Locally the tomb was known as 'the grave of the seven times married one.'

You'd be forgiven for thinking it was Bluebeard's grave; he was reputed to have killed several wives in turn because they showed undue curiosity about a locked room. But this was the tomb of Susanna Anna-Maria Yeates, and the inscription (most of it in Latin) stated that she was mourned by all who had benefited from her generosity, her beneficiaries having included various schools, orphanages, and the church across the road. There was no sign of any other graves in the vicinity and presumably her husbands had been interred in the old Rajpur graveyard, below the Delhi Ridge.

I was still in my teens when I first saw the ruins of what had once been a spacious and handsome mansion. Desolate and silent, its well-laid paths were overgrown with weeds, and its flower beds had disappeared under a growth of thorny jungle. The two-storeyed house had looked across the Grand Trunk Road. Now abandoned, feared and shunned, it stood encircled in mystery, reputedly the home of evil spirits.

Outside the gate, along the Grand Trunk Road, thousands of vehicles sped by—cars, trucks, buses, tractors, bullock carts—but few noticed the old mansion or its mausoleum, set back as they were from the main road, hidden by mango, neem and peepul trees. One old and massive peepul tree grew out of the ruins of the house, strangling it much as its owner was said to have strangled one of her dispensable paramours.

As a much-married person with a quaint habit of disposing of her husbands whenever she tired of them, Susanna's malignant spirit was said to haunt the deserted garden. I had examined the tomb, I had gazed upon the ruins, I had scrambled through shrubbery and overgrown rose bushes, but I had not encountered the spirit of this mysterious woman. Perhaps, at the time, I was too pure and innocent to be targeted by malignant spirits. For malignant she must have been, if the stories about her were true.

The vaults of the ruined mansion were rumoured to contain a buried treasure—the amassed wealth of the lady Susanna. But no one dared go down there, for the vaults were said to be occupied by a family of cobras, traditional guardians of buried treasure. Had she really been a woman of great wealth, and could treasure still be buried there? I put these questions to Naushad, the furniture-maker, who had lived in the vicinity all his life, and whose father had made the furniture and fittings for this and other great houses in Old Delhi.

'Lady Susanna, as she was known, was much sought after for her wealth,' recalled Naushad. 'She was no miser, either. She spent freely, reigning in state in her palatial home, with many horses and carriages at her disposal. Every evening she rode through the Roshanara Gardens, the cynosure of all eyes, for she was beautiful as well as wealthy. Yes, all men sought her favours, and she could choose from the best of them. Many were fortune hunters. She did not discourage them. Some found favour for a time, but she soon tired of them. None of her husbands enjoyed her wealth for very long!

'Today no one enters those ruins, where once there was mirth and laughter. She was the Zamindari lady, the owner of much land, and she administered her estate with a strong hand. She was kind if rents were paid when they fell due, but terrible if someone failed to pay.

'Well, over fifty years have gone by since she was laid to rest, but still men speak of her with awe. Her spirit is restless, and it is said that she often visits the scenes of her former splendour. She has been seen walking through this gate, or riding in the gardens, or driving in her phaeton down the Rajpur road.'

'And what happened to all those husbands?' I asked.

'Most of them died mysterious deaths. Even the doctors were baffled. Tomkins Sahib drank too much. The lady soon tired of him. A drunken husband is a burdensome creature, she was heard to say. He would eventually have drunk himself to death, but she was an impatient woman and was anxious to replace him. You see those datura bushes growing wild in the grounds? They have always done well here.'

'Belladonna?' I suggested.

'That's right, huzoor. Introduced in the whisky-soda, it put him to sleep for ever.'

'She was quite humane in her way.'

'Oh, very humane, sir. She hated to see anyone suffer. One sahib, I don't know his name, drowned in the tank behind the house, where the water lilies grew. But she made sure he was half-dead before he fell in. She had large, powerful hands, they said.'

'Why did she bother to marry them? Couldn't she just have had men friends?'

'Not in those days, huzoor. Respectable society would not have tolerated it. Neither in India nor in the West would it have been permitted.'

'She was born out of her time,' I remarked.

'True, sir. And remember, most of them were fortune hunters. So we need not waste too much pity on them.'

'*She* did not waste any.'

'She was without pity. Especially when she found out what they were really after. Snakes had a better chance of survival.'

'How did the other husbands take their leave of this world?'

'Well, the Colonel sahib shot himself while cleaning his rifle. Purely an accident, huzoor. Although some say she had loaded his gun without his knowledge. Such was her reputation by now that she was suspected even when innocent. But she bought her way out of trouble. It was easy enough, if you were wealthy.'

'And the fourth husband?'

'Oh, he died a natural death. There was a cholera epidemic that year, and he was carried off by the *haija*. Although, again, there were some who said that a good dose of arsenic produced the same symptoms! Anyway it was cholera on the death certificate. And the doctor who signed it was the next to marry her.'

'Being a doctor, he was probably quite careful about what he ate and drank.'

'He lasted about a year.'

'What happened?'

'He was bitten by a cobra.'

'Well, that was just bad luck, wasn't it? You could hardly blame it on Susanna.'

'No, huzoor, but the cobra was in his bedroom. It was coiled around the bedpost. And when he undressed for the night, it struck! He was dead when Susanna came into the room an hour later. She had a way with snakes. She did not harm them and they never attacked her.'

'And there were no antidotes in those days. Exit the doctor. Who was the sixth husband?'

'A handsome man. An indigo planter. He had gone bankrupt when the indigo trade came to an end. He was hoping to recover his fortune with the good lady's help. But our Susanna mem, she did not believe in sharing her fortune with anyone.'

'How did she remove the indigo planter?'

'It was said that she lavished strong drink upon him, and when he lay helpless, she assisted him on the road we all have to take by pouring molten lead in his ears.'

'A painless death, I'm told.'

'But a terrible price to pay, huzoor, simply because one is no longer needed . . .'

We walked along the dusty highway, enjoying the evening breeze, and some time later we entered the Roshanara Gardens, in those days Delhi's most popular and fashionable meeting place.

'You have told me how six of her husbands died, Naushad. I thought there were seven?'

'Ah the seventh was a gallant young magistrate who perished right here, huzoor. They were driving through the park after dark when the lady's carriage was attacked by brigands. In defending her, the young man received a fatal sword wound.'

'Not the lady's fault, Naushad.'

'No, huzoor. But he was a magistrate, remember, and the assailants, one of whose relatives had been convicted by him, were out for revenge. Oddly enough, though, two of the men were given employment by the lady Susanna at a later date. You may draw your own conclusions.'

'And were there others?

'Not husbands. But an adventurer, a soldier of fortune came along. He found her treasure, they say. And he lies buried with it, in the cellars of the ruined house. His bones lie scattered there, among gold and silver and precious jewels. The cobras guard them still! But how he perished was a mystery, and remains so till this day.'

'And Susanna? What happened to her?'

'She lived to a ripe old age. If she paid for her crimes, it wasn't in this life! She had no children, but she started an orphanage and gave generously to the poor and to various schools and institutions, including a home for widows. She died peacefully in her sleep.'

'A merry widow,' I remarked. 'The Black Widow spider!'

Don't go looking for Susanna's tomb. It vanished some years ago, along with the ruins of her mansion. A smart new housing estate came up on the site, but not after several workmen and a contractor succumbed to snake bite! Occasionally residents complain of a malignant ghost in their midst, who is given to flagging down cars, especially those driven by single men. There have also been one or two mysterious disappearances.

And after dusk, an old-fashioned horse and carriage can sometimes be seen driven through the Roshanara Gardens. If you chance upon it, ignore it, my friend. Don't stop to answer any questions from the beautiful fair lady who smiles at you from behind lace curtains. She's still looking for her final victim.

The Amorous Servant

The only servant I ever had for any length of time was Kundan Singh.

Why I took him on, and why I kept him, I do not really know, for I never cared much for him. He was not very efficient, he ate more than most people, borrowed money, gambled in the bazaars, drank raw country liquor, and usually overslept in the mornings.

When Kundan Singh first came to me for a job, I thought he looked unreliable. He had a dull, rather expressionless face, and eyes that refused to meet mine.

However, he addressed me as 'sahib'—this was the first time I had received this title, and it immediately made me feel important—and told me he could cook, wash dishes, make a garden and cut trees. As I was living at the time in a small room in a crowded city area, I had no garden and the nearest tree was a mile distant. Nevertheless, I thought I could do with a cook and general factotum. And what pleased me in Kundan Singh was that he had absolutely no references.

In those days, most domestic servants carried around with them a number of 'chits'—letters from former employers, testifying to the solid worth and honesty of the servant whom they were so ready to be rid of. Not only did I distrust these chits, but I disliked their worn, tattered appearance. They made one think of a graduate carrying his bachelor's degree around in his pocket. Kundan Singh had never heard of 'chits', and this pleased me. It meant he had not worked in a very posh household, and that I would not, therefore, have to consider myself his inferior. Either that, or it meant he had been dismissed from all his previous positions.

Kundan, who was eighteen (at a rough guess), told me he had no parents, no relatives at all. He had apparently been sent out into the world while still a child, and had been expected to send money orders home every month. This he never did; and learning after a few years that his parents were dead, he shrugged his shoulders fatalistically. He had never wanted to return to his village in the hills, where there were no cinemas, no liquor shops, and no diversions of any sort.

He soon settled in with me. He liked my irregular hours, and he liked the absence of any real work. It was possible for him to go to a picture in the evening, and return the next morning, and not be taken to task. He knew that I liked a cup of tea while I was still in bed, and he saw that I got it, because that guaranteed that I would be in a tolerant mood for the rest of the day.

I was paying Kundan Singh thirty rupees a month, with food—of which he ate at least another thirty rupees' worth. He generally asked for his pay in advance, and spent it before the month was halfway through.

It was only after Kundan had been with me a couple of months that I realized he had a weakness for women—or, to be more accurate, that women had a weakness for him.

This surprised me, because I did not think of him as being very passionate. He struck me as being rather Teutonic in his indifferent approach to sex. But apparently there were mysterious fires smouldering beneath Kundan's rather drab exterior; and women, I suppose, are good at sensing these things.

He told me the woman was a relative, his uncle's sister. She must have been his senior by about ten years. Her face and figure were mature, but I do not know if she had any children. She was not attractive by our effeminate modern standards. Her ears, due to the heavy rings in them, were large and shapeless; her nose and mouth were rather broad. But she had that generous female form which is so rare nowadays: full, pendulous breasts, broad hips and substantial thighs. She spent several nights with Kundan on the veranda, and I assumed that her interest in the youth was purely maternal. I was not very interested, except to warn Kundan that he would have to feed her out of his own rations.

It was only when the woman's husband turned up and made a scene, that I realized she was Kundan's lover and not his relative. Her composure was admirable. She stood calmly while her husband raved and Kundan expostulated. Thankfully, they did not come to blows. The man demanded twenty rupees as a salve for his injured pride, and Kundan asked me if I could advance him the money. This I did, in order to be rid of them. The woman turned up again the following day and I told Kundan he would have to keep her somewhere else.

'What do you see in her?' I asked him. 'She is much older than you.'

'I cannot escape her, sahib,' said Kundan. 'She follows me everywhere. She is like a man-eating tigress and it is impossible for a weakling like me to satisfy her. Sometimes she torments me even after I am completely spent. Even her husband cannot manage her. She has taken a fancy to me, I don't know why. But she says, sahib, that you are very good-looking. Would you be interested . . .'

'No,' I said firmly. I did not think I could afford an adventure, especially one in which the husband had also to be rewarded from time to time.

I think Kundan was a little disappointed in me. I was a little disappointed myself.

Kundan's next liaison was with the daughter of the local butcher. It was a clandestine affair, conducted in all sorts of impossible places—behind the garbage dump, or in dark alleys behind the shops—and it came to an abortive end when the butcher got wind of the affair and threatened Kundan with immediate castration.

Inspite of Kundan's amorous and amoral exploits, I was quite happy with him. He was a good cook, and he did not boss me. He was lazy, as most amorous creatures are; but then, so was I. Fortunately, he lazed while I worked, and worked while I lazed. It was the perfect master-servant relationship. As a friend once remarked to me, 'I notice you have a guest living with you these days.'

Unfortunately all good things must come to an end, and my rather aimless existence in the city was one of them. I told Kundan that I would be going away and that I would no longer be requiring his services.

He seemed genuinely distressed.

'Sahib,' he said. 'You are my father and my brother and my mother. Please take me with you.'

'I can't afford to,' I said. 'But I will try to get you another job.'

I spoke to the owner of a small restaurant where I had occasionally taken a meal. He was a middle-aged man who had developed a paunch through sitting for long hours on the raised platform behind his glass cases of Indian sweets. His first wife, who had been issueless, was dead. Recently he had been married again to a young woman from the hills. As is the custom in many hill areas, he had paid the parents of the girl the sum of two thousand rupees. The restaurant, situated near a cinema, did good business, and the proprietor could afford the luxury of a young wife.

On my recommendation, he employed Kundan on a salary of forty rupees a month. The young man was loth to take the job, and kept insisting he would accompany me to the ends of the earth. But I finally persuaded him to leave me, and he began working at the restaurant the same day I left the city.

It was six years before I returned to the city. My travelling job had brought me to a town in its vicinity, and for sentimental reasons I decided to revisit the place where I had spent so many delightfully wasted years. There were of course old friends to meet, and it was only after I had been in the city a couple of days, and was passing the familiar restaurant, that I remembered Kundan Singh. So I stepped into the restaurant, to be greeted effusively by the proprietor.

He had grown fatter and lazier—but then, so had I. Kundan, he told me, had left after working in the restaurant for only a year. He had no idea where the young man had gone—probably back to his village, or into the army.

I was having a cup of strong tea with the proprietor when a child, a boy of about five, ran into the restaurant. The proprietor beamed with paternal affection and introduced the boy to me as his son.

'Your first?' I asked.

'Yes, the only one,' he said proudly. 'But he is the equal of five ordinary sons. See, isn't he healthy? He looks just like his mother.' He pinched the boy's chubby arms and ruffled his hair. 'But I wish he would pay more attention to his books. As you know, sir, there is no future for a young man who does not get his degree.'

'Surely it's too early to be thinking of a degree for him?'

The proprietor assured me that it was never too early to think of acquiring credentials; but I wasn't listening to him very carefully. There was something about the boy which I found familiar and striking. His narrow forehead, slanting eyes, and crooked little smile reminded me of someone . . . Kundan Singh! I sat up with a start and looked at the proprietor, but could see no resemblance to the boy . . .

Of course it was only the vaguest suspicion, and I kept my mouth shut. I had never seen the proprietor's wife, and it was quite possible that she closely resembled my former servant. After all, they came from the same hill region. I had nothing to go on but a resemblance, and in any case it was impossible to ask too many questions. The proprietor himself had no suspicions: he said the boy looked like his mother. Why worry? The child was being well spoilt, and would grow up to possess both a degree and a restaurant.

I never did visit the city again, and I never met Kundan.

But last year, thumbing through a military journal, I came across several pages of photographs of young soldiers who had died in a heroic action on India's northern borders. Amongst them I recognised my former servant. He sported a moustache, and his hair had been cropped close; but there was no mistaking his lean, hungry look.

I could not help feeling rather proud of Kundan Singh. And a little envious. His youth had been free and easy, he had sown his wild oats and before he could become old and decrepit and useless, he had died a hero. That is something very few of us are able to achieve.

Monkey Trouble

Grandfather bought Tutu from a street entertainer for the sum of ten rupees. The man had three monkeys. Tutu was the smallest but the most mischievous. She was tied up most of the time. The little monkey looked so miserable with a collar and chain that Grandfather decided it would be much happier in our home. He had a weakness for keeping unusual pets. It was a habit that I, at the age of eight or nine, used to encourage.

Grandmother at first objected to having a monkey in the house. 'You have enough pets as it is,' she said, referring to Grandfather's goat, several white mice, and a small tortoise.

'But I don't have any,' I said.

'You're wicked enough for two monkeys. One boy in the house is all I can take.'

'Ah, but Tutu isn't a boy,' said Grandfather triumphantly. 'This is a little girl monkey!'

Grandmother gave in. She had always wanted a little girl in the house. She believed girls were less troublesome than boys. Tutu was to prove her wrong.

She was a pretty little monkey. Her bright eyes sparkled with mischief beneath deep-set eyebrows. And her teeth, which were a pearly white, were often revealed in a grin that frightened the wits out of Aunt Ruby, whose nerves had already suffered from the presence of Grandfather's pet python in the house at Lucknow. But this was Dehra, my grandparents' house, and aunts and uncles had to put up with our pets.

Tutu's hands had a dried-up look, as though they had been pickled in the sun for many years. One of the first things I taught her was to shake hands, and this she insisted on doing with all who visited the house. Peppery Major Malik would have to stoop and shake hands with Tutu before he could enter the drawing room, otherwise Tutu would climb on his shoulder and stay there, roughing up his hair and playing with his moustache.

Uncle Ken couldn't stand any of our pets and took a particular dislike to Tutu, who was always making faces at him. But as Uncle Ken was never in a job for long, and depended on Grandfather's good-natured generosity, he had to shake hands with Tutu like everyone else.

Tutu's fingers were quick and wicked. And her tail, while adding to her good looks (Grandfather believed a tail would add to anyone's good looks), also served as a third hand. She could use it to hang from a branch, and it was capable of scooping up any delicacy that might be out of reach of her hands.

Aunt Ruby had not been informed of Tutu's arrival. Loud shrieks from her bedroom brought us running to see what was wrong. It was only Tutu trying on Aunt Ruby's petticoats! They were much too large, of course, and when Aunt Ruby entered the room all she saw was a faceless white blob jumping up and down on the bed.

We disentangled Tutu and soothed Aunt Ruby. I gave Tutu a bunch of sweet peas to make her happy. Granny didn't like anyone plucking her sweet peas, so I took some from Major Malik's garden while he was having his afternoon siesta.

Then Uncle Ken complained that his hairbrush was missing. We found Tutu sunning herself on the back verandah, using the hairbrush to scratch her armpits. I took it from her and handed it back to Uncle Ken with an apology; but he flung the brush away with an oath.

'Such a fuss about nothing,' I said. 'Tutu doesn't have fleas!'

'No, and she bathes more often than Ken,' said Grandfather, who had borrowed Aunt Ruby's shampoo for giving Tutu a bath.

All the same, Grandmother objected to Tutu being given the run of the house. Tutu had to spend her nights in the outhouse, in the company of the goat. They got on quite well, and it was not long before Tutu was seen sitting comfortably on the back of the goat, while the goat roamed the back garden in search of its favourite grass.

The day Grandfather had to visit Meerut to collect his railway pension, he decided to take Tutu and me along—to keep us both out of mischief, he said. To prevent Tutu from wandering about on the train, causing inconvenience to passengers, she was provided with a large black travelling bag. This, with some straw at the bottom, became her compartment. Grandfather and I paid for our seats, and we took Tutu along as hand baggage.

There was enough space for Tutu to look out of the bag occasionally, and to be fed with bananas and biscuits, but she could not get her hands through the opening and the canvas was too strong for her to bite her way through.

Tutu's efforts to get out only had the effect of making the bag roll about on the floor or occasionally jump into the air—an exhibition that attracted a curious crowd of onlookers at the Dehra and Meerut railway stations.

Anyway, Tutu remained in the bag as far as Meerut, but while Grandfather was producing our tickets at the turnstile, she suddenly poked her head out of the bag and gave the ticket collector a wide grin.

The poor man was taken aback. But, with great presence of mind and much to Grandfather's annoyance, he said, 'Sir, you have a dog with you. You'll have to buy a ticket for it.'

'It's not dog!' said Grandfather indignantly. 'This is a baby monkey of the species macacus-mischievous, closely related to the human species homus-horriblis! And there is no charge for babies!'

'It's as big as a cat,' said the ticket collector.

'Next you'll be asking to see her mother,' snapped Grandfather.'

In vain did he take Tutu out of the bag. In vain did he try to prove that a young monkey did not qualify as a dog or a cat or even as a quadruped. Tutu was classified as a dog by the ticket collector, and five rupees were handed over as her fare.

Then Grandfather, just to get his own back, took from his pocket the small tortoise that he sometimes carried about, and said: 'And what must I pay for this, since you charge for all creatures great and small?'

The ticket collector looked closely at the tortoise, prodded it with his forefinger, gave Grandfather a triumphant look, and said, 'No charge, sir. It is not a dog!'

Winters in north India can be very cold. A great treat for Tutu on winter evenings was the large bowl of hot water given to her by Grandmother for a bath. Tutu would cunningly test the temperature with her hand, then gradually step into the bath, first one foot, then the other (as she had seen me doing) until she was in the water up to her neck.

Once comfortable, she would take the soap in her hands or feet and rub herself all over. When the water became cold she would get out and run as quickly as she could to the kitchen fire in order to dry herself. If anyone laughed at her during this performance, Tutu's feelings would be hurt and she would refuse to go on with the bath.

One day Tutu almost succeeded in boiling herself alive. Grandmother had left a large kettle on the fire for tea. And Tutu, all by herself and with nothing better to do, decided to remove the lid. Finding the water just warm enough for a bath, she got in, with her head sticking out from the open kettle.

This was fine for a while, until the water began to get heated. Tutu raised herself a little out of the kettle. But finding it cold outside, she sat down again. She continued hopping up and down for some time until Grandmother returned and hauled her, half-boiled, out of the kettle.

'What's for tea today?' asked Uncle Ken gleefully. 'Boiled eggs and a half-boiled monkey?'

But Tutu was none the worse for the adventure and continued to bathe more regularly than Uncle Ken.

Aunt Ruby was a frequent taker of baths. This met with Tutu's approval—so much so, that one day, when Aunt Ruby had finished shampooing her hair she looked up through a lather of bubbles and soapsuds to see Tutu sitting opposite her in the bath, following her example.

One day Aunt Ruby took us all by surprise. She announced that she had become engaged. We had always thought Aunt Ruby would never marry—she had often said so herself—but it appeared that the right man had now come along in the person of Rocky Fernandes, a schoolteacher from Goa.

Rocky was a tall, firm-jawed, good-natured man, a couple of years younger than Aunt Ruby. He had a fine baritone voice and sang in the manner of the great Nelson Eddy. As Grandmother liked baritone singers, Rocky was soon in her good books.

'But what on earth does he see in her?' Uncle Ken wanted to know.

'More than any girl has seen in you!' snapped Grandmother. 'Ruby's a fine girl. And they're both teachers. Maybe they can start a school of their own.'

Rocky visited the house quite often and brought me chocolates and cashewnuts, of which he seemed to have an unlimited supply. He also taught me several marching songs. Naturally I approved of Rocky. Aunt Ruby won my grudging admiration for having made such a wise choice.

One day I overheard them talking of going to the bazaar to buy an engagement ring. I decided I would go along too. But as Aunt Ruby had made it clear that she did not want me around I decided that I had better follow at a discreet distance. Tutu, becoming aware that a mission of some importance was under way, decided to follow me. But as I had not invited her along, she too decided to keep out of sight.

Once in the crowded bazaar, I was able to get quite close to Aunt Ruby and Rocky without being spotted. I waited until they had settled down in a large jewellery shop before sauntering past and spotting them as though by accident. Aunt Ruby wasn't too pleased at seeing me, but Rocky waved and called out, 'Come and join us! Help your aunt choose a beautiful ring!'

The whole thing seemed to be a waste of good money, but I did not say so—Aunt Ruby was giving me one of her more unloving looks.

'Look, these are pretty!' I said, pointing to some cheap, bright agates set in white metal. But Aunt Ruby wasn't looking. She was immersed in a case of diamonds.

'Why not a ruby for Aunt Ruby?' I suggested, trying to please her.

'That's her lucky stone,' said Rocky. 'Diamonds are the thing for engagement.' And he started singing a song about a diamond being a girl's best friend.

While the jeweller and Aunt Ruby were sifting through the diamond rings, and Rocky was trying out another tune, Tutu had slipped into the shop without being noticed by anyone but me. A little squeal of delight was the first sign she gave of her presence. Everyone looked up to see her trying on a pretty necklace.

'And what are those stones?' I asked.

'They look like pearls,' said Rocky.

'They are pearls,' said the shopkeeper, making a grab for them.

'It's that dreadful monkey!' cried Aunt Ruby. 'I knew that boy would bring him here!'

The necklace was already adorning Tutu's neck. I thought she looked rather nice in them, but she gave us no time to admire the effect. Springing out of our reach Tutu dodged around Rocky, slipped between my legs, and made for the crowded road. I ran after her, shouting to her to stop, but she wasn't listening.

There were no branches to assist Tutu in her progress, but she used the heads and shoulders of people as springboards and so made rapid headway through the bazaar.

The jeweller left his shop and ran after us. So did Rocky. So did several bystanders who had seen the incident. And others, who had no idea what it was all about, joined in the chase. As Grandfather used to say, 'In a crowd, everyone plays follow-the-leader even when they don't know who's leading.'

She tried to make her escape speedier by leaping on to the back of a passing scooterist. The scooter swerved into a fruit stall and came to a standstill under a heap of bananas, while the scooterist found himself in the arms of an indignant fruitseller. Tutu peeled a banana and ate part of it before deciding to move on.

From an awning she made an emergency landing on a washerman's donkey. The donkey promptly panicked and rushed down the road, while bundles of washing fell by the wayside. The washerman joined in the chase. Children on their way to school decided that there was something better to do than attend classes. With shouts of glee, they soon overtook their panting elders.

Tutu finally left the bazaar and took a road leading in the direction of our house. But knowing that she would be caught and locked up once she got home, she decided to end the chase by riding herself of the necklace. Deftly removing it from her neck, she flung it in the small canal that ran down that road.

The jeweller, with a cry of anguish, plunged into the canal. So did Rocky. So did I. So did several other people, both adults and children. It was to be a treasure hunt!

Some twenty minutes later, Rocky shouted, 'I've found it!' Covered in mud, water lilies, ferns and tadpoles, we emerged from the canal, and Rocky presented the necklace to the relieved shopkeeper.

Everyone trudged back to the bazaar to find Aunt Ruby waiting in the shop, still trying to make up her mind about a suitable engagement ring.

Finally the ring was bought, the engagement was announced, and a date was set for the wedding.

'I don't want that monkey anywhere near us on our wedding day,' declared Aunt Ruby.

'We'll lock her up in the outhouse,' promised Grandfather. 'And we'll let her out only after you've left for your honeymoon.'

A few days before the wedding I found Tutu in the kitchen helping Grandmother prepare the wedding cake. Tutu often helped with the cooking, and, when Grandmother wasn't looking, added herbs, spices, and other interesting items to the pots—so that occasionally we found a chilli in the custard or an onion in the jelly or a strawberry floating on the chicken soup.

Sometimes these additions improved a dish, sometimes they did not. Uncle Ken lost a tooth when he bit firmly into a sandwich which contained walnut shells.

I'm not sure exactly what went into that wedding cake when Grandmother wasn't looking—she insisted that Tutu was always very well-behaved in the kitchen—but I did spot Tutu stirring in some red chilli sauce, bitter gourd seeds, and a generous helping of eggshells!

It's true that some of the guests were not seen for several days after the wedding but no one said anything against the cake. Most people thought it had an interesting flavour.

The great day dawned, and the wedding guests made their way to the little church that stood on the outskirts of Dehra—a town with a church, two mosques, and several temples.

I had offered to dress Tutu up as a bridesmaid and bring her along, but no one except Grandfather thought it was a good idea. So I was an obedient boy and locked Tutu in the outhouse. I did, however, leave the skylight open a little. Grandmother had always said that fresh air was good for growing children, and I thought Tutu should have her share of it.

The wedding ceremony went without a hitch. Aunt Ruby looked a picture, and Rocky looked like a film star.

Grandfather played the organ, and did so with such gusto that the small choir could hardly be heard. Grandmother cried a little. I sat quietly in a corner, with the little tortoise on my lap.

When the service was over, we trooped out into the sunshine and made our way back to the house for the reception.

The feast had been laid out on tables in the garden. As the gardener had been left in charge, everything was in order. Tutu was on her best behaviour. She had, it appeared, used the skylight to avail of more fresh air outside, and now sat beside the three-tier wedding cake, guarding it against crows, squirrels and the goat. She greeted the guests with squeals of delight.

It was too much for Aunt Ruby. She flew at Tutu in a rage. And Tutu, sensing that she was not welcome, leapt away, taking with her the top tier of the wedding cake.

Led by Major Malik, we followed her into the orchard, only to find that she had climbed to the top of the jack-fruit tree. From there she proceeded to pelt us with bits of wedding cake. She had also managed to get hold of a bag of confetti, and when she ran out of cake she showered us with confetti.

'That's more like it!' said the good-humoured Rocky. 'Now let's return to the party, folks!'

Uncle Ken remained with Major Malik, determined to chase Tutu away. He kept throwing stones into the tree, until he received a large piece of cake bang on his nose.

Muttering threats, he returned to the party, leaving the Major to do battle.

When the festivities were finally over, Uncle Ken took the unnecessary old car out of the garage and drove up to the verandah steps. He was going to drive Aunt Ruby and Rocky to the nearby hill resort of Mussoorie, where they would have their honeymoon.

Watched by family and friends, Aunt Ruby and Rocky climbed into the back seat. Aunt Ruby waved regally to everyone. She leant out of the window and offered me her cheek and I had to kiss her farewell. Everyone wished them luck.

As Rocky burst into song Uncle Ken opened the throttle and stepped on the accelerator. The car shot forward in a cloud of dust.

Rocky and Aunt Ruby continued to wave to us. And so did Tutu from her perch on the rear bumper! She was clutching a bag in her hands and showering confetti on all who stood in the driveway.

'They don't know Tutu's with them!' I exclaimed. 'She'll go all the way to Mussoorie! Will Aunt Ruby let her stay with them?'

'Tutu might ruin the honeymoon,' said Grandfather. 'But don't worry—our Ken will bring her back!'

Colonel Wilkie's Good Hunting

Colonel Wilkie and I set off into the foothills on a cold, dew-fresh February morning, while the Siwaliks were still shrouded in mist. The Colonel, wearing an old Army bush shirt and khaki trousers, carried his .12-bore shotgun. I carried his walking stick, which I handed to him whenever the going was difficult. Ahead of us, or sometimes behind us as the mood took him, ran the Colonel's gun dog, Flash, a young spaniel who had been trained to flush out birds for the benefit of his master.

The Colonel was in his early sixties, and lived on a pension. He had been a good shot in his younger days, and his veranda walls were decorated with the mounted heads of gazelles, antelope, wild buffalo and snow leopard, all shot at different times and places during his long sojourn in India.

Advancing years, an arthritic arm, and the high cost of good whisky, had all combined to spoil the Colonel's aim. When inviting me to be his house guest for a week, he had promised me a partridge shoot, and he wasn't one to break his promises. Though I would gladly have foregone the shoot (for I hate early risings), I remembered that the Colonel had oiled and cleaned his gun the night before, and I did not want to disappoint him.

'This is the right sort of country for partridge,' he said, as he exchanged his gun for his walking stick in order to surmount a steep bank. 'Plenty of scrub, and fields not far off. That suits 'em nicely. But there's not much else, I'm afraid. The deer were shot out years ago.'

We had not gone far when Flash raised his head and sniffed into the wind.

'He's scented them,' said the Colonel, 'Go, send them up, boy!'

Flash ran ahead with his nose to the ground, and disappeared into a thicket of lantana bushes. As he did so, a covey of partridges whirred up from the bushes. The Colonel dropped his walking stick, grabbed his gun, raised it to his shoulder, and blazed away.

Not one of the birds fell. They flew low over the bushes, swept round the contour of the hill, and then settled down again about a furlong away.

'Bad luck,' I said.

'Too damned far,' said the Colonel. 'Out of range. Good boy, Flash,' he said, as the dog came back in high spirits. 'We'll get 'em yet.'

Forgetting his stick, Colonel Wilkie set off across the mustard field, calling Flash to heel whenever the dog showed signs of running too far ahead. When we were well into the field, the Colonel allowed the dog to run on.

Flash certainly knew his job. The birds took to the air again, and the Colonel blasted off another barrel.

He missed by yards. The partridges flew swift and low over the field, and settled down less than a hundred yards away. They had been shot at by the Colonel on previous occasions, and were secure in the knowledge that he invariably missed.

Flash came back, his stumpy tail gyrating with pleasure. He did not expect anything wonderful from the Colonel, but he was enjoying himself.

'It's these damned cartridges,' grumbled Colonel Wilkie, now rather red in the face. 'They're absolutely no good—the shot just bounces off those birds!'

'Never mind,' I said. 'Have another go. They're not far off.'

We advanced further into the mustard field, muddying our boots and trousers, while Flash went tearing off through the flowering yellow mustard. Up rose the birds. Up went Colonel Wilkie's gun. Off went both barrels, one immediately after the other.

To the amazement of everyone—Colonel Wilkie, Flash, the partridges and myself—one of the birds plummeted to the ground.

'Good shot, sir!' I cried.

'Go fetch it, Flash!' shouted the Colonel with delight. And to me, 'Roast partridge for supper, old boy!'

He was as pleased as if he had just shot his first partridge. I could not help sharing in his enthusiasm.

Flash bounded forward. He'd had plenty of experience in flushing out birds, but this was the first time, since graduating from the Saharanpur Kennel Club, that he had been called upon to retrieve one. Perhaps that was why his next act was out of keeping with the character of a gun dog.

He picked the bird up in his mouth, and then, instead of bringing it back to us, made off with the precious trophy!

'Flash, come back at once!' cried Colonel Wilkie. 'The silly dog thinks the bird was meant for him!'

'Well, perhaps he deserves it,' I said.

'And so do I—deserve it,' snapped the Colonel, adding, in a rare moment of frankness, 'First partridge I've shot for years. Ever since this arm started giving me trouble . . .'

We trudged home through the fields, still faintly hoping that Flash would be waiting for us with the bird intact. But we were disappointed. The dog came home two hours later, looking very guilty, with a few partridge feathers stuck to the sides of his mouth.

'Well, he certainly hasn't wasted anything,' I observed.

The Colonel was too fond of his dog to think of punishing him. But, for several minutes, polite civilian formality gave way to some good old Army profanity, and several new words were added to my vocabulary.

The Family Ghost

'Now tell us a ghost story,' I told Bibiji, my landlady,
evening, as she made herself comfortable on the old couch
in the veranda. 'There must have been at least one ghost in
your village.'

'Oh, there were many,' said Bibiji, who never tired of
telling us weird tales. 'Wicked *churels* and mischievous
prets. And there was a *munjia* who ran away.'

'What is a munjia?' I asked.

'A munjia is the ghost of a brahmin youth who had
committed suicide on the eve of his marriage. Our village
munjia had taken up residence in an old peepul tree.'

'I wonder why ghosts always live in peepul trees!' I
said.

'I'll tell you about that another time,' said Bibiji. 'But
listen to the story about the munjia . . .'

Near the village peepul tree (according to Bibiji) there
lived a family of brahmins who were under the special
protection of this munjia. The ghost had attached himself

to this particular family (they were related to the girl to whom he had once been betrothed) and showed his fondness for them by throwing stones, bones, night soil and rubbish at them, making hideous noises, and terrifying them whenever he found an opportunity. Under his patronage, the family soon dwindled away. One by one they died, the only survivor being an idiot boy, whom the ghost did not bother, because he thought it beneath his dignity to do so.

But, in a village, birth, marriage and death must come to all, and so it was not long before the neighbours began to make plans for the marriage of the idiot.

After a meeting of the village elders, they agreed, first, that the idiot should be married; and second, that he should be married to a shrew of a girl who had reached the age of sixteen without finding a suitor.

The shrew and the idiot were soon married off, and then left to manage for themselves. The poor idiot had no means of earning a living and had to resort to begging. Previously, he had barely been able to support himself, and now his wife was an additional burden. The first thing she did when she entered his house was to give him a box on the ear and send him out to bring something home for their dinner.

The poor fellow went from door to door, but nobody gave him anything, because the same people who had arranged his marriage were annoyed that he had not given them a wedding feast. When, in the evening, he returned home empty-handed, his wife cried out, 'Are you back, you lazy idiot? Where have you been so long, and what have you brought for me?'

When she found he hadn't even a paisa, she flew into a rage and, tearing off his turban, threw it into the peepul tree. Then, taking up her broom, she thrashed her husband until he fled from the house, howling with pain.

But the shrew's anger had not yet diminished. Seeing her husband's turban in the peepul tree, she began to beat the tree trunk, accompanying her blows with strong abuses. The ghost who lived in the tree was sensitive to her blows and, alarmed that her language might have the effect of finishing him off altogether, he took to his invisible heels, and left the tree on which he had lived for many years.

Riding on a whirlwind, the ghost soon caught up with the idiot who was still running down the road leading away from the village.

'Not so fast, brother!' cried the ghost. 'Desert your wife, certainly, but not your old family ghost! The shrew has driven me out of my peepul tree. Truly, a ghost is no match for a woman with a vile tongue! From now on we are brothers and must seek our fortunes together. But first promise me that you will not return to your wife.'

The idiot made this promise very willingly, and together they continued their journey until they reached a large city.

Before entering the city, the ghost said, 'Now listen, brother, and if you follow my advice, your fortune is made. In this city there are two very beautiful girls, one is the daughter of a Raja, and the other the daughter of a rich moneylender. I will go and possess the daughter of the Raja and her father will try every sort of remedy without effect. Meanwhile you must walk daily through the streets in the robes of a sadhu, and when the Raja comes and asks you to cure his daughter, make any terms that you think suitable. As soon as I see you, I shall leave the girl. Then I shall go and possess the daughter of the moneylender. But do not go anywhere near her, because I am in love with the girl and do not intend giving her up. If you come near her, I shall break your neck.'

The ghost went off on his whirlwind, and the idiot entered the city on his own, and found a bed in the local rest house for pilgrims.

The next day the city was agog with the news that the Raja's daughter was dangerously ill. Physicians—*hakims* and *vaids*—came and went, and all pronounced the girl incurable. The Raja was distracted with grief, and offered half his fortune to anyone who would cure his beautiful and only child. The idiot, having smeared himself with dust and ashes, began walking the streets, occasionally crying out: '*Bhum, bhum, bho! Bom Bhola Nath!*'

The people were struck by his appearance, and taking him for a wise and holy man, reported him to the Raja. The latter immediately entered the city and, prostrating himself before the idiot, begged him to cure his daughter. After a show of modesty and reluctance, the idiot was persuaded to accompany the Raja back to the palace, and the girl was brought before him.

Her hair was dishevelled, her teeth were chattering, and her eyes almost starting from their sockets. She howled and cursed and tore at her clothes. When the idiot confronted her, he recited certain meaningless spells; and the ghost, recognizing him, cried out: 'I go I go! *Bhum, bhum, bho!*'

'Give me a sign that you have gone,' demanded the idiot.

'As soon as I leave the girl,' said the ghost, 'you will see that mango tree uprooted. That is the sign I'll give.'

A few minutes later, the mango tree came crashing down. The girl recovered from her fit, and seemed unaware of what had happened to her. The news spread through the city, and the idiot became an object of respect and wonder. The Raja kept his word and gave him half his fortune; and so began a period of happiness and prosperity for the idiot.

A few weeks later, the ghost took possession of the moneylender's daughter, with whom he was deeply in love. Seeing his daughter go out of her right senses, the moneylender sent for the highly esteemed idiot and offered him a great sum of money if he would cure his daughter. But remembering the ghost's warning, the idiot refused to go. The moneylender was enraged and sent his henchmen to bring the idiot to him by force; and the idiot, having no means of resisting, was dragged along to the rich man's house.

As soon as the ghost saw his old companion he cried out in a rage: 'Idiot, why have you broken our agreement and come here? Now I will have to break your neck!'

But the idiot, whose reputation for wisdom had actually served to make him wiser, said, 'Brother ghost, I have not come to trouble you, but to tell you a terrible piece of news. Old friend and protector, we must leave this city soon. You see, SHE has come here—my dreaded wife, the shrew!—to torment us both, and to drag us back to the village. She is on the road to this house and will be here in a few minutes!'

When the ghost heard this, he cried out: 'Oh no, oh no! If she has come, then we must go! *Bhum bho, bhum bho*, we go, we go!'

And breaking down the walls and doors of the house, the ghost gathered himself up into a little whirlwind and went scurrying out of the city, to look for a vacant peepul tree.

The moneylender, delighted that his daughter had been freed of the evil influence, embraced the idiot and showered presents on him. And in due course, concluded Bibiji, the idiot married the moneylender's beautiful daughter, inherited his father-in-law's wealth and became the richest and most successful moneylender in the city.

Living Without Money

When I was in my twenties, there were a number of us who lived without electric light—not because there was no electricity, but because no one had paid their bills.

Dehra was going through a slump in those days, and there wasn't much work for anyone—least of all for my neighbour, Suresh Mathur, income-tax lawyer, who was broke for two reasons. To begin with, clients were a rarity, as those with taxable incomes were few and far between; apart from that, when he did get work, he was slow and half-hearted about getting it done. This was because he seldom got up before eleven in the morning, and by the time he took a bus down from Rajpur and reached his own small office, or the Income Tax Office a little further on, it was lunchtime and all the tax officials were out. Suresh would then repair to the Royal Café for a beer or two (often at my expense) and this would stretch into a gin and tonic, after which he would stagger up to his first-floor office and collapse on the sofa for an afternoon nap. He would wake up at six, after the income-tax office had closed.

I occupied two rooms next to his office, and we were on friendly terms, sharing an enthusiasm for the humorous works of P.G. Wodehouse. I think he modelled himself on Bertie Wooster, for he would often turn up wearing mauve or yellow socks or a pink shirt and a bright green tie—enough to make anyone in his company feel quite liverish. But unlike Bertie Wooster, he did not have a Jeeves to look after him and get him out of various scrapes with creditors, bookmakers or clients who felt he'd let them down. I was a bit wary of Suresh, as he was in the habit of borrowing lavishly from all his friends, conveniently forgetting to return the amounts. I wasn't well off and could ill afford the company of a spendthrift friend.

Looking back, I am amazed at the number of people who were quite broke. There was William Matheson, a Swiss journalist, whose remittances from Zurich never seemed to turn up; my landlady, whose husband had deserted her two years previously; Mr Madan, who dealt in second-hand cars which no one wanted; the owner of the corner restaurant, who sat in solitary splendour surrounded by empty tables; and the proprietor of the Ideal Book Depot, who was selling off his stock of books so he could convert his depot into a department store. We complain that few people buy or read books today, but I can assure you that there were even fewer customers in the fifties and sixties. It seemed only doctors, dentists and the proprietors of English schools were making money.

Suresh had an advantage over the rest of us—he owned an old bungalow, inherited from his father, up at

Rajpur in the foothills, where he lived alone with an old manservant. And owning a property gave him some standing with his creditors. The grounds boasted of a mango and lichee orchard, and these he gave out on contract every year. The proceeds helped him to pay his office rent in town, with a little left over to give small amounts on account to the owner of the Royal Café.

If a lawyer could be hard up, what chance had a journalist? And yet William Matheson had everything going for him when he came out to India as an assistant to Von Hesseltein, a correspondent for some of the German papers. Von Hesseltein passed on some of his assignments to William, and for a time all went well. William lived with Von Hesseltein and his family, and was also friendly with Suresh, often paying for the drinks at the Royal Café. Then William committed the folly (if not the sin) of sleeping with Von Hesseltein's wife. He justified this indiscretion by telling us that Von Hesseltein was sleeping with the malai-wala, a strapping young man in his twenties who was a great advertisement for the invigorating qualities of malai. William obviously felt that Von Hesseltein's wife was getting a raw deal. But Von Hesseltein was not the understanding sort. He threw William out of the house and stopped giving him work.

William hired an old typewriter and set himself up as a correspondent in his own right, living and working from a room in the Doon Guest House. He bombarded the Swiss and German papers with his articles, but there were very few takers. No one then was really interested in India's five-year plans, or Corbusier's Chandigarh, or the Bhakra-Nangal Dam. Book publishing in India was confined to textbooks, otherwise William might have published a vivid account of his experiences in the French Foreign Legion. After two or three rums at the Royal Café he would regale us with tales of his exploits in the Legion, before and after the siege of Dien-Bien-Phu. Some of his stories had the ring of truth, others (particularly his sexual exploits) were obviously tall tales; but never the less I was happy to pay for the beer or coffee in order to hear him spin them out.

I was living off my own literary endeavours, selling stories and articles to the Indian papers (about half a dozen scattered throughout the country), with the occasional sale of a story to the BBC or *Young Elizabethan*, a children's magazine published in the UK. In those days there was a greater market for essays and short fiction, so my early stories found a home more easily then than they do today.

Those were glorious days for Ruskin Bond, unknown freelance writer. I was realizing my dream of living by my pen, and I was doing it from a small town in north India, having turned my back on both London and New Delhi. I had no ambitions to be a great writer, or even a famous one, or even a rich one. All I wanted to do was *write*. And I wanted a few readers and the occasional cheque so that I could carry on living my dream.

The cheques came along in their own desultory way—fifty rupees from the *Weekly*, or thirty-five from *The Statesman* or the same from *Sport and Pastime*, and so on—just enough to get by and to be the envy of Suresh Mathur, William Matheson and a few others, professional people who felt that I had no business earning more than they did. Suresh even declared that I should have been paying tax, and offered to represent me, his other clients having gone elsewhere.

Colonel Wilkie did not earn anything either. He lived on a small pension in a corner room of the White House Hotel. His wife had left him some years before, presumably because of his drinking, but he claimed to have left her because of her obsession with moving the furniture: it seems she was always shifting things about, changing rooms, throwing out perfectly sound tables and chairs and replacing them with fancy stuff picked up here and there. If he took a liking to a particular easy chair and showed signs of settling down in it, it would disappear the next day to be replaced by something horribly ugly and uncomfortable.

'It was a form of mental torture,' said Colonel Wilkie, confiding in me over a glass of beer on the White House veranda. 'The sitting room was cluttered with all sorts of ornamental junk and flimsy side tables, and I was constantly falling over the damn things. It was like a minefield! And the mines were never in the same place. You've noticed that I walk with a limp?'

'First World War?' I ventured. 'Wounded at Ypres? Or was it Flanders?'

'Nothing of the sort,' snorted the Colonel. 'I did get one or two flesh wounds but they were nothing as compared to the damage inflicted on me by those damned shifting tables and chairs. Fell over a coffee table and dislocated my shoulder. Then broke an ankle negotiating a stool that was in the wrong place. Bookshelf fell on me. Tripped on a rolled-up carpet. Hit by a curtain rod. Would you have put up with it?'

'No,' I had to admit.

'Had to leave her, of course. She went off to England. Send her an allowance. Half my pension! All spent on furniture!'

The Colonel told me that the final straw had come when his favourite spring bed had suddenly been replaced by a bed made up of hard wooden slats. It was sheer torture trying to sleep on it, and he had left his house and moved into the White House Hotel as a permanent guest.

Now he had gone to the other extreme and wouldn't allow anyone to touch or tidy up anything in his room. There were beer-stains on the tablecloth, cobwebs on his family pictures, dust on his books, empty medicine bottles on his dressing table and mice nesting in his old, discarded boots.

I didn't see much of the room because we usually sat out on the veranda, waited upon by one of the hotel bearers, who came over with bottles of beer that I dutifully paid for, the Colonel having exhausted his credit. I suppose he was in his late sixties then. He never went anywhere, not even for a walk in the compound. He blamed this inactivity on his gout, but it was really inertia and an unwillingness to leave the precincts of the bar, where he could cadge the occasional drink from a sympathetic guest.

Colonel Wilkie had given up on life. I suppose he could have gone off to England, but he would have been more miserable there, with no one to buy him a drink (since he wasn't likely to reciprocate), and the possibility of his wife turning up again to rearrange the furniture.

No one arranged my furniture. I didn't have any, except for my bed and an old dining table which served as my writing desk. My landlady was Dehra's first lady shopkeeper. She was a very large woman with poor eyesight and high blood pressure. But she gave me an excellent breakfast—stuffed parathas with shalgam pickle, which sustained me through most of the day. In the evenings I ate at a dhaba near the Orient Cinema, a little way down the road.

The Orient was one of Dehra's older cinemas, started in the 1930s by a Parsi, Mr Gazder, who had since passed on. Over the entrance it had a couple of eye-catching frescoes of dancers, created by Sudhir Khastgir, the Doon School's art master. The cinema, where as a boy I saw Abbot and Costello comedies, and classics such as *Key Largo* and *The Maltese Falcon*, switched over to Hindi movies in the 1950s and later to soft porn—films with exotic titles such as *Dark Blue Nights* and *Bedroom Follies*, purported to be foreign but actually made down south.

Some of my younger friends, from Karanpur and the Dilaram Bazaar, occasionally accompanied me to the pictures and often invited me to their homes. These boys were, in fact, far more hospitable than people like Suresh Mathur or William Matheson, who were always cash-strapped. In the Dilaram area there were Narinder and Sahib Singh, whose mothers were always feeding me. And in Karanpur there was Sudheer, whose father owned a small press from which he issued a newspaper called *The Frontier Mail*. I would occasionally help with the paper, correcting proofs and editing contributions; it was valuable experience.

Apart from a mutual liking, these youngsters admired me because I'd made a name for myself at the age of twenty-one—barely two or three years older than they were—something my older friends (Suresh and William and others) couldn't quite come to terms with.

All the same, after two years of freelancing in Dehra, I found that my income remained static and I wasn't really making much headway as an author. One novel published in England hadn't really put me on the literary map. I was discontented with myself. There I was, stagnating in the Doon, supplementing my income with English tuitions and correcting proofs for *The Frontier Mail*! I could probably have continued in this mode for several years, and might even have been a better writer for it, but a job in Delhi beckoned, and I thought it might be to my advantage to make a move.

So I packed my bags (all my belongings fit quite easily into two suitcases) and took an early morning bus to Delhi, promising my young friends that I would come back with my fortune made! The Dilaram boys, ever loyal, remained in touch with me, and even turned up in Delhi from time to time, but I had no news of Suresh or William or the Colonel—and it was to be three years before I found myself in Dehra again.

Delhi in the 1960s wasn't really my sort of place. The refugee influx from Pakistan had resulted in many far-flung residential complexes springing up in arid areas where there was no form of entertainment or cultural activity. To obtain a book I had to travel all the way from Rajouri Gardens to Connaught Place (forty-five minutes in a bus); and if I wanted to meet a like-minded friend, it was another forty minutes by Delhi Transport to the Civil Lines in Old Delhi.

How I longed for Dehra's little Royal Café, and those idle hours with Suresh Mathur and Co. How I missed my bicycle-riding friends from the Dilaram Bazaar. And Dehra's little bookshops, and the lichee trees, and my lamp-lit room above my landlady's homely provision store.

I longed to return, but I'd taken up a job with a relief agency and they were paying me quite well. I felt I had to stick it out for a couple of years before making another bid for freedom, the sort of freedom that only successful freelancing could bring me. My time in Delhi was not a creative period; I travelled without absorbing much; I was writing project reports instead of stories.

When, after three and a half years, I did revisit my old home town, I took a room at the White House Hotel. Colonel Wilkie was missing. He had died of cirrhosis the previous year, and had been given a simple burial by those who knew him. A few weeks after the funeral his wife turned up and went through his effects, selling most of his few possessions to the local kabadi-wala. She hadn't liked the location of his grave and had wanted to shift it, in the manner of her furniture, but the local padre had refused. She had gone off in a huff, without paying for a tombstone, so the Colonel's grave remained unmarked.

William had left the Doon. According to reliable reports, he had inherited his father's wealth back in Switzerland, and was now married to a beauty from Guatemala who was working her way through his fortune. I had a feeling he'd turn up again some day, asking me for a small loan.

Good old Suresh had also had a stroke of luck, although I suppose it should really be attributed to good management on his part. The year after I'd gone away he had sold his Rajpur house to a middle-aged widowed princess; he had then struck up a close friendship with her and a year later they were married. When I met him in the Royal Café, I told him he'd made a smart move, a remark which seemed to offend him: he assured me that he was genuinely in love with the princess. And he paid for the beer and told me that the house was up for sale again! Apparently they were thinking of moving to Delhi.

Everyone was moving out of Dehra, including my Dilaram Bazaar friends. Dehra was a place where you could get by, but there were no career prospects for young men, no 'further education' (whatever that meant), and no real business opportunities. It was a good place to go to school, but after graduating, many chose to seek their fortune elsewhere. Only the odd fellow like me came back—briefly.

I wanted to live in Dehra again, and I thought seriously about it; but I kept putting it off. And when eventually, I'd had enough of Delhi, I looked for a retreat in the hills, where I could write and be myself and even fall in love from time to time.

So here I am, forty years on, perched on a hilltop overlooking the valley where I grew up and grew into a writer. And sometimes I go down to the valley, not to look up old friends (for all of them have gone their different ways) but simply to try and recapture the feel of the place as I knew it.

It has changed, of course, as places must over a period of time. A small garden town has grown into a large town without gardens. Not quite a city, although it comes close to being one, with its congested roads, polluting traffic and overburdened civic structure. A few lichee orchards remain but most have been replaced by housing estates. Here and there a shopkeeper recognizes me. Some of the old buildings are still here, with peepal trees growing out of the walls. The great maidan has shrunk, encroached upon by bus stands, motor workshops, and a clutter of makeshift structures. There are people everywhere. The population has gone from 50,000 in 1950 to over 700,000 at the coming of the millennium. There are pockets of prosperity; there is money to be made in the marketplace; but the unemployed and the unemployable will soon by vying for standing room.

But here's a quiet corner. A nice old building with a patch of grass in front . . . Ah, it's the old White House Hotel! A bit run-down now, like the rest of us survivors from that era, but I can still find lodging for the night . . . And in the morning I shall sit on the veranda where a frond of bougainvillaea trails, and write this little memoir.